BLOODY MARY CONFESSION

JACK ERICKSON

REDBRICK PRESS

BLOODY MARY CONFESSION

Jack Erickson
Copyright © 2024 by Jack Erickson

ALL RIGHTS RESERVED

This is a work of fiction based upon the imagination of the author. No real people are represented.

ISBN: 978-0-941397-24-7

Sign up for Erickson's newsletter at:

www.RedBrickPress.net

www.JackErickson.com

Follow Erickson's international travel at A Year and a Day.

Jack Erickson's books are available on all digital sites and at www.RedBrick-Press.net

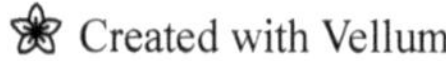 Created with Vellum

CONTENTS

DEDICATION

To the Class of 1962 Williston Coyotes

ALSO BY JACK ERICKSON

Milan Thriller Series

Thirteen Days in Milan
No One Sleeps
Vesuvius Nights
The Lonely Assassin

Novels
Bloody Mary Confession
Rex Royale
A Streak Across the Sky
Mornings Without Zoe

Short Mysteries
Perfect Crime
Missing Persons
Teammates
The Stalker
Weekend Guest

True Crime
Blood and Money in the Hunt Country

Noir Series
Bad News is Back in Town

Political Satire
The Next President of the United States

Audio Books
Perfect Crime
The Stalker
A Streak Across the Sky

Nonfiction
Star Spangled Beer:
A Guide to America's New Microbreweries and Brewpubs
Great Cooking with Beer
Brewery Adventures in the Wild West
California Brewin'
Brewery Adventures in the Big East

1

BLOODY MARY CONFESSION
Jack Erickson

The Bison of North Dakota State University beat the University of North Dakota Sioux 24-17 the last weekend of October in my junior year. It was a big upset. NDSU had suffered through a miserable 2-7 season, but we beat our biggest rival, the conference champion from Grand Forks, eighty miles north of Fargo.

The Bison defense had swarmed through UND's backfield, trapping halfbacks and sacking their star quarterback six times. Our noodle-armed senior quarterback had surprised everyone and played the best game of his collegiate career—three touchdown passes, twenty-one completions, 289 yards passing, and no interceptions.

After the gun went off to end the fourth quarter, my date and I ran onto the field with other students, celebrating as if we'd won the Rose Bowl. The crowd pulled down the goalposts, tore chunks of the field as souvenirs, and surrounded our team in their mud- and grass-stained uniforms. It had rained in the morning, and the teams had chewed up the turf until the field looked like a World War I's no-man's-land by the end of the game.

The Bison marching band played the school fight song as it circled the team in the center of the field. The university president handed over the Nickel Trophy to our coach for winning the annual grudge match between NDSU and UND. The aluminum trophy, two inches thick and nearly two feet in diameter, is a replica of a nickel coin. We were ecstatic that "the slug" would be returned to the student union trophy case from which it had been absent for four years.

The stadium lights dimmed as our team, surrounded by cheering students and the marching band, headed for the locker room. Crowds shuffled toward the exits and into the jammed parking lots, where campus police were directing traffic into two lanes, one leading to the highway and the other downtown to University Avenue, where thirsty fans, voices raw from cheering, were pouring into bars to celebrate the upset.

My sexy freshman date, Tika, and I got stuck in traffic and didn't get onto the highway until the stadium was dark. We joined a horn-honking caravan of trucks, cars, and minibuses headed to a postgame beer blast at the ranch of my fraternity brother Cliff Westbrook half an hour west of Fargo.

"Wish you were playing football, Max?" Tika asked as she nuzzled next to me in my truck, the back window of which was plastered with fraternity and NDSU stickers. "You were a football star in high school, weren't you?" She put a hand on my thigh and squeezed.

"Yeah, I played quarterback. I love football, but I made a good choice to play baseball instead."

To be honest, I was envious of the football team, many of

whom were friends from the athletic dorm where I lived. I'd been offered a football scholarship to NDSU after I'd quarter-backed my high school team in Williston, North Dakota, to the state championship my senior year. I'd also been offered a base-ball scholarship, and I'd had to make a choice.

After talks with both coaches, I had chosen the baseball scholarship. My dream was to play professional sports, and I felt I was twenty pounds too light and two inches too short to get drafted into the NFL. But I was the right size and speed to play second base and make it into the major leagues.

"I can't wait for baseball season, Max," Tika said. "My sorority sisters say you're the best player on the team."

"Aah, they're just teasing you," I said. "We have a lot of good players on the team. We might make it to the College World Series. We almost made it last year, but our pitching staff fell apart at the end of the season, and our center fielder broke his shoulder slamming against a fence at the conference tournament."

"I'll bet you're the best-looking player on the team." Tika was a fun date but sometimes acted like she was still in high school, which she had been in May.

The caravan drove west from Fargo on I-90 to a turnoff that led to the Triple Rock ranch. We climbed a small hill and then descended to where we could see the lights of the Westbrook ranch house, barns, and corral. The ranch house was set back in a grove of oak trees and had a backyard swimming pool where we had partied after baseball games.

Paper sacks with burning candles inside lined the road to a parking lot by the barn, stable, and corrals across from the ranch house. Yard lights lit up the corral, where hay bales had been set up for the party. A bonfire blazed in the center. A small herd of Black Angus cattle in a neighboring corral stared at us, their large, sad eyes shining in the light of the flames.

Fraternity pledges collected ten dollars per person as we

filed into the corral and headed to the beer kegs. A six-foot stack of logs blazed in the center of the corral, shooting glowing embers and smoky ropes into the cold October evening air. The chilly temperature accented the rural autumn aroma of freshly cut hay, cow manure, bonfire smoke, and beer flowing from kegs.

The crowd was mostly athletes and members of NDSU fraternities and sororities. They crowded into the corral and sat on hay bales, drinking beer, waving school banners, and singing off-key to Queen's "We Are the Champions" blasting from a boom box.

After getting beer from a keg, Tika and I joined my fraternity brothers at the grill, where bowls of chili were being spooned from cooking pots and cheeseburgers were being dished up. We drenched our cheeseburgers with ketchup, mustard, and relish and headed to the hay bales to knock back our beers and wolf down the food.

While we were celebrating, Cliff's parents came out of their ranch house to mingle with the crowd, slapping backs, shaking hands, and joining the fun. One of the brothers handed them foaming beer cups, which they raised, to the cheers of the noisy, drunken crowd. When there was a break in the music, someone yelled, "Let's hear it for Hank and Louise! Thanks for letting us shake up the ranch!"

"Whoo . . . whoo . . . whoo," the crowd chanted, spilling beer from cups as they weaved around the roaring bonfire.

"Hank! Hank! Louise! Louise! You're the greatest! Whoo! Whoo! Whoo!"

Hank looked like you'd expect a North Dakota rancher to look on a cold October evening. He wore a red deer hunter's vest over a flannel shirt, jeans with a horseshoe-shaped belt buckle, cowboy boots, and a Stetson creased and soiled from years of ranching.

Louise was attractively thin and dressed stylishly in a tan

pantsuit. Gaudy silver bracelets decorated her wrists, and she wore rings the size of gumballs.

Hank got up on a hay bale and held up his beer. "Have fun, kids. Just be safe. If you can't drive home tonight, we've got plenty of room in the old bunkhouse."

"Whoo . . . whoo . . . whoo! Hank and Louise! We beat the Sioux!"

After Hank got down from the hay bale, he and Louise made their way around the corral, chatting and reminiscing about their good times at NDSU. Nice folks. Good Midwestern stock.

The party rolled on. The Rolling Stones blasted out "Satisfaction" and "Brown Sugar" from the boom box, beer flowed, the crowd celebrated, and everyone was getting a little drunk.

The autumn sky was ablaze with a million stars. It was a night when you believed you would live forever and catch every break in life. Everyone was your best friend. Every sorority girl wanted to jump in the sack with you. Fraternity brothers would be your friends for life. Your body would never fail you. Nothing could ever go wrong. Our dreams, good looks, health, fortune, luck, and popularity would last forever.

The callowness of youth.

Tika was the hottest new bauble on campus. She had been homecoming queen at her high school and had dated the football star. She was a model of Midwestern purity, with long Scandinavian blonde hair, sparkling blue eyes, and a pinup's body. She was as feisty as a den of puppies. She didn't walk; she bounced.

Every guy had been hot on Tika's trail when she showed up on campus in September. She went through sorority rush and told the sisters she was going to be faithful to her football star boyfriend, who was a freshman at Northwestern. She bragged that they would be getting engaged the following summer and would marry after their sophomore years, when she would transfer to Northwestern.

Tika told the sisters that she would date but just wanted to be "friends" with fraternity guys. She went out with a different one almost every night; all they got at the end of the evening was a kiss on the cheek or a handshake.

Tika told me this on our first date. I smiled and said, "It's nice to know who you are going to marry when you're eighteen, Tika. I hope it works out for you."

We slept together after our third date, and Tika never mentioned her Northwestern boyfriend again. So much for a freshman coed's convictions.

Whenever I took Tika to fraternity parties, guys rolled their eyes and gave me an envious look. "Man, how did you get lucky with Tika? I took her out three times and only got a peck on the cheek! Whaddaya got that I don't, Max?"

I'd smile, shrug my shoulders, and say, "No idea. Don't have a clue."

Cupcakes like Tika had been dropping into my lap since I was sixteen. I had been a jock, lettering in football, basketball, and baseball at Williston High School. My grades were good, and I was decent looking. But nothing thrilled teenage girls more than when they saw me throw a touchdown pass, sink a jump shot, or hit a home run. I suppose you could say I took advantage of that.

When I'd arrived at NDSU, I'd stumbled into paradise, bumping into drop-dead-gorgeous coeds in class, at parties, in bars, and especially at the library. That's where the smartest coeds hung out. Beauty and brains—my favorite type.

But after a few tumbles in the sack, my fickle eye would wander. I'd spot another delicious treat and move on. Rejection and doubt never clouded my psyche. That would come later.

The night air was getting chillier, and the crowd inched closer to the bonfire. I stepped away from Tika and headed over to the kegs to get more beer. Tika was back by the corral fence, talking to a brother and his date, scanning the crowd for me. I raised my foaming beer cup to signal where I was. She waved and turned back to continue talking. She looked delicious, her ample breasts bulging in a tight green and gold sweater, our team colors.

The bonfire was roaring, its flames licking higher into the cold, black night sky and disappearing in the flicker of twinkling stars. After I'd refilled our beer cups, I was making my way through the crowd when I bumped into someone wearing a blue sweatshirt.

"Oh—sorry. Sorry," I muttered as she turned around.

"Max! Howya doin', guy? Great game! Whoo! Whoo!"

It was Debra Marcum, a classmate who'd been subtly hitting on me in marketing class.

"Hey, Debra, great to see you!" I shouted above the raucous laughter.

Debra stood on her toes and yelled in my ear. "We beat the Sioux! Yeah!" she slurred, her eyes glazed.

"Wasn't it great?" I shouted back. Debra snuggled closer, pressing against my arm.

I'd bantered with Debra in class, but she wasn't my type. She was on a golf scholarship, a sport that didn't appeal to me. She was from Chicago and wore jerseys and sweatshirts of the Cubs, Bears, Bulls, and Blackhawks. I like a woman to dress like a woman: tight slacks, an attractive blouse, and makeup to accent her feminine features. Debra was wearing a Chicago Bears sweatshirt. The ties from its hood dangled on her breasts, which were buried in the bulky sweatshirt.

Almost everyone on campus knew Debra, but I hadn't seen her with a date before. She was like one of the guys, not someone you'd take to a party. Between classes you'd find her in the memorial union coffee shop, where jocks gathered, talking sports trash or telling dirty jokes. When everyone got up to go to class, she'd be left alone.

Debra was decent looking but wore glasses with red frames like a comedian would wear. However, I liked her. She was sassy to professors when she thought they were being lazy or patronizing. She debated with them in class and often made her point, to the delight of the other students.

"You alone tonight, hot stuff?" she asked, giving me "that look." She wanted a roll in the hay, and I was in her sights.

"Naw, I've got a date, Debra. Sorry."

"Damn!" she said, wrinkling her puppy nose. "You with that blonde freshman with melon boobs and stork legs?"

"Yeah, I'm with Tika."

She rolled her eyes. "Where on God's earth did Tika get that flaky name? What the hell does it mean?"

The Talking Heads started up with "Burning Down the House." The drunken crowd shouted the lyrics off-key.

"It was the first word she said when she was a baby," I shouted above the singing. "She called everything 'Tika'—her parents, a cup, a spoon, her dog. She'd crawl around the house saying 'Tika . . . Tika . . . Tika.' Kinda cute, isn't it?"

Debra groaned and squeezed my arm, almost making me spill a beer. "Max, that's sooo lame! Damn, you ballplayers are all the same. All testosterone, crotch-grabbing, and chest-thumping."

"Come on, Debra. You know that's not me."

"Yeah, I know. I like you because you've got a brain behind those killer eyes and wavy hair."

"Tika's a wholesome girl. Goes to church. Calls her parents every Sunday," I drawled in my faux country boy dialect. "Daddy's a lawyer and mom's a nurse. Salt of the earth."

Debra tipped back her head and laughed. "Max! You're not interested in Tika's bloodlines. You like her bedroom gymnastics! She's your latest conquest. By the time the snow flies, you'll find another star-struck freshman to drag into your cave."

Debra's eyes widened. She said, "Hey, did you get all those mixed metaphors? I should repeat that in English class and watch the professor have a heart attack!"

"Debra, baby," I drawled, "you make me sound like a cad."

"Aah, don't worry. I still love ya, Max," she slurred, planting a wet kiss on my cheek. "Can I give you a tip?"

"Sure."

"You're a real catch. Don't waste your time with guppies. Tika's just a plaything. You need a real woman—someone who can stimulate you intellectually, not just tickle your toy. Contrary to what you think, your brain is your most attractive organ," she said, giving me a lascivious grin and looking down at my crotch.

A coed weaving through the crowd came up and greeted Debra. "Hey, Deb, great to see you here. How ya been?" She was wearing an NDSU varsity jacket over a V-neck sweater showing delicious cleavage. My blood pressure spiked.

I'd seen her around campus and been intrigued by her distinguished features; honey-blonde hair brushed back over her head, almond-shaped eyes, a creamy complexion, and high cheekbones. Her smile would melt steel.

"Hey, Amanda," Debra said. "You look great tonight, honey. You with Karl?" They exchanged a perfunctory hug.

Amanda pointed toward the corral gate, where the basketball team was in a circle. "Sure thing. Karl's with the basketball team. They're initiating a transfer student. This is the last weekend before practice starts Monday. Then it's curfew every night and no beer."

"Can they have sex before curfew?" Debra asked, poking Amanda in the side with her elbow.

Amanda winked. "Well, the coach says they need to save their strength to win games. But, you know, some rules are made to be broken."

Debra and Amanda hooted, high-fived with bare hands, and sipped their beers. Debra looked at me. "Max, you know Amanda Foxx? She's dating Karl Helmken, our star forward. Karl averaged eighteen points a game last year. Made second all-conference team."

Fitting. Amanda Foxx. She was a fox. I reached out with my free hand to Amanda. She laid hers in mine and gave me a gentle squeeze. Her hand was warm and soft like a kitten's paw. I didn't want to let it go.

"Hi, Amanda. I'm Max," I said, trying to sound relaxed. "Karl's the best player on the team. He has a great close-in jump shot and hits the board like a pro. He's going to have a great season."

"That ain't all the talent Karl has, from what I hear. He's prime stud," Debra said, leering at Amanda.

Amanda didn't respond. Debra recognized her social faux pas and shifted gears, putting a hand on my arm. "Max's my marketing class buddy."

"Pleasure to meet you, Max." She was taller than Debra, an inch or two shorter than I was. I like tall women. Especially tall, sexy ones.

Amanda was more than beautiful; she had the distinctive appearance of a classic movie actress from a bygone era. Lauren Bacall. Sophia Loren. Deborah Kerr. A presence. An air of mystery. An allure that made you want to know everything about her. I couldn't take my eyes off her.

"Max is one of the smart jocks," Debra said. "He plays second base and gets good grades. He'll play in the majors one day and become a professor when he retires."

Amanda looked at me and said in a sexy drawl, "You date Tika, right, Max? I remember her from rush. Cute girl." Her deep-set eyes were pale green, the color of a leaf in spring.

"That's right."

When she smiled at me, I felt glowing coals warming my heart. I wanted to hear her talk so I could continue to look into her eyes.

"I've heard about you," she said in an intimate tone, almost as if we were at a sidewalk cafe and not at a college beer bash. "You dated Rochelle last spring during baseball season."

"That's right."

"She's in my drama class. She said you're a fun guy, great at parties, and a good dancer."

"Funny and smart," Debra chimed in, sensing she was being left out. "He knows how to pitch products. He gave a Power-Point presentation on marketing toiletries with sports themes."

"Really? That sounds creative," Amanda said, raising her eyebrows. "Pitch me, Max. Show me your stuff."

Tika could wait. Amanda had my attention. "I'm not a pitcher. I play second base."

"Come on now, you know what I mean," she said wrinkling her nose. "Pitch me a line tonight, Max. You up for it?"

"What do you want me to pitch?"

She sipped her beer, looking over the rim at me. "Pitch yourself." Our eyes were locked like we were the only people on the planet. "I want to hear how you charmed Debra."

I was challenged by her directness; with a challenge comes the chance for a reward. What was mine going to be?

"I can do that," I said, inching closer to Amanda until I could smell the beer on her breath and a whiff of an intoxicating perfume. I hoped she couldn't hear my heart thumping against my chest.

"I'm all ears," she teased in a sultry drawl. We'd met a minute ago, but I wanted to grab her and drive off into the dark night.

"Whoa, it's getting hot here," Debra teased, fanning a hand in front of her face. "Could it be the bonfire? Or is something else going on?"

This was an opportunity I wasn't going to miss. The bonfire was blazing nearby. Fraternity brothers and their dates were singing bawdy songs and pouring down beers. But none of that mattered; Amanda and I were two planets speeding toward each other, destined to collide in an explosion of fire, hot gases, and molten metal. We both knew it.

I needed to be on my "A" game. I wasn't going for a single; I wanted a home run.

"Baseball is the greatest sport in the world," I started, wondering where the hell I was going with this.

A corner of Amanda's mouth curled in a sly grin, her teeth sparkling in the glow of the bonfire. "Ooh, I like baseball, Max. You've got my attention. Why is baseball the greatest sport?"

I sipped my beer, building the suspense. "Baseball appeals to our animal brain, where we have our deepest emotions."

"Tell me more about our animal brain," she said, cocking her head in a playful gesture.

Her voice had dropped to a sultry whisper. She had me right where she wanted, a toy to play with. I was being seduced by a master.

I waited for a lull in the drunken singing. I was winging it and had to think fast. "Our animal brain is where our spirit lives." Oh, God, did that sound as weak as I thought?

"I'm into the spirit thing," she said, wrinkling her nose again. "Tell me more."

Maybe it wasn't such a weak opening after all.

"Our animal brain is linked to survival, whether we're in the jungle or flying a supersonic fighter."

"Ooh, Max," Debra groaned, "it's getting high and deep!" her eyes darted back and forth between Amanda and me.

Amanda gave me a beery smile. "I'm with you. Keep talking, Max." A tease, a delicious tease. I loved it. We were playing games at a kegger, a little drunk, full of mischief. I shifted gears.

"A baseball diamond is a thing of beauty and symmetry. Three bases and home plate equal distance from each other, laid out in a diamond. A pitcher's mound sixty feet from home plate, a circular dirt pulpit surrounded by emerald green grass. Beyond the infield, the outfield is bordered by arrow-straight white chalk lines separating fair territory from foul. The brain likes that beauty and precision.

Amanda smiled. "I see a baseball diamond as an outdoor theater. The team on the field is onstage; the team in the dugout is waiting to go onstage. You could say baseball is a drama. Or even a ballet, with all the graceful, athletic moves each player displays."

Debra and I were momentarily speechless from Amanda's interpretation. "Interesting," I said, wondering if I could run with Amanda's analogy. "Baseball is a drama. When the batter hits a long fly ball and the outfielder catches it, the crowd roars like an audience cheering an actor."

Amanda raised a fist in affirmation. "True. But if the outfielder doesn't catch the ball, the crowd moans like when an actor on stage reveals a shocking line that twists the plot." Touché.

This was fun. I had to think fast to keep our word game going. "And if the batter hits a long fly ball, the crowd is standing, cheering and hoping that it will be a home run."

"Yes!" Amanda said, pumping her fist. "And if it is, they give the batter a standing ovation. Like a curtain call at the end of a play."

"Exactly!" I emphasized, clenching my fist and bumping hers. "And each play on the diamond, or on stage, only lasts seconds."

"A few seconds is all it takes to change the game," she said, sipping her beer, our eyes locked. "Like life, isn't it, Max?"

"It is. A few seconds can change everything."

We were all quiet for a moment, as if we had finished a scene in a play but the audience hadn't yet moved on.

"Wow. It's not Shakespeare, but you two click!" Debra said, clenching her fist and bumping ours. "A mini sports drama in a corral with the ripe odor of fresh horse manure, keg beer, and a bonfire to make it memorable."

We all sipped silently from our beers, not wanting to spoil the moment, a moment we'd remember far beyond that evening.

I knew I'd fall asleep that night remembering Amanda's face glowing in the light of the bonfire, our spontaneous verbal match, our not taking our eyes off each other.

Amanda said, "Thanks for introducing us, Debra."

She turned to me and put her hand on my arm. "You're funny —and cute, Max." Shivers ran all over my body. "A jock with brains. My favorite type."

2

———

Debra rolled her eyes at me when I walked into our ten o'clock marketing class Monday morning. She was sitting at the back of the class, her feet sticking out in front of her, wearing a Chicago Cubs sweatshirt, jeans, and running shoes. Her hair was tied back in a ponytail; she most likely had slept late and hadn't had time to put on makeup.

When I sat down next to her, she punched my arm and gave me a "you sly old dog" look. "Hey, hot stuff, you hit a grand slam Saturday night," she said. "Amanda's got the hots for you. When you went back to Tika, she swooned like a lovesick hound dog. 'God, is he cool!' she told me. I told her you were the real thing, gorgeous and brainy."

I hadn't been able to get Amanda out of my mind the rest of the weekend. "Thanks for the introduction," I said, feeling a little self-conscious with her flattery.

"You owe me, big fellow. Buy me coffee after class. I got a hot tip for you about Amanda."

"Sure thing."

"It's not free. I want a payback."

"What's that?"

She patted me on the cheek and said, "Don't worry, it won't cost you a penny. When you make it to the majors, I want front-row tickets to your first game and a signed baseball."

"Deal," I said with a smile. "You sound convinced I'll make it."

"Of course you will! You told me at the beginning of the semester that was your dream. So go do it! What's stopping you?" Nothing subtle about Debra. I liked that about her.

After class, Debra and I walked out of the business building onto the campus lawn. It was a sunny, cool October morning. the sky as blue and luscious as in a Manet painting.

The business school was one of four red brick buildings that enclosed the campus quad, the others being the education, technology, and engineering departments. The campus lawn was layered in a carpet of gold, red, yellow, and orange leaves that had fallen from the oak and maple trees in the quad. Our feet crunched through the leafy carpet as we breathed in the autumn aroma of fallen leaves. We stopped at the fountain in the center of the quad, a popular hangout between classes.

Each fraternity and sorority had staked out areas around the fountain where they socialized, smoked cigarettes, flirted, and talked about the weekend football game and parties. I spent a couple of minutes talking with my fraternity brothers while looking around to see if Amanda was there. She hadn't shown up there before, and I wondered why.

Debra and I left the fountain and walked towards the campus bookstore and cafeteria, another popular place between classes. I bought us coffee and she staked out a table in the corner as students filed out on their way to classes.

"You were hotter than a pistol on Saturday," she said as we sipped our coffee. "I haven't felt such sexual tension since Han and Leia met in *Star Wars*. Did you think about dumping Tika and taking Amanda back to campus?"

I looked at her in mock horror. "Debra, I'd never do something so caddish. Of course I took Tika back; she was my date. I'm a gentleman."

She gave me a lascivious grin. "Maybe so, big boy, but I know where your fantasies were headed. Good thing I was standing off to the side Saturday night. I could have been seriously injured when your libidos collided."

We both laughed. Debra was an incurable teaser with teachers, classmates, and the jocks she hung out with.

"So," she continued, "what do you know about Amanda other than that you two set off fireworks like it was the Fourth of July?"

"Not much, really. I know she's dating Karl."

"Do you know her major?"

"No. Should I?"

"When you see her next time—and I know like God made green apples that you will—you could rack up points if you did. She's a drama major."

"Hmm, interesting. That's why she made the drama references Saturday night. I don't know anyone else in drama. That's probably why I never see her at the fountain."

"Right. The drama building is behind the ag building, across from the parking lot."

"I've never been there."

"Let me give you a tip so you can make a good second impression. As if you need one, which you don't."

"I'd appreciate it."

"She's in a drama class's production of *His Girl Friday* opening this weekend. One of my friends works backstage. She says Amanda's a pretty fine actress."

"What's the play about?"

"A comedy about reporters at a prison waiting for an execution."

"It's a comedy?"

"It was a play on Broadway and was made into a movie with

Cary Grant and Rosalind Russell. I saw it in rehearsal last week; it's a scream. Amanda plays the Russell part. Funny and sexy at the same time. From what my sorority sister says, comedy's one of the hardest roles for an actor or actress to play."

"Maybe I should go."

"Take Tika. Let her see the competition."

"Competition?" I said with a hint of mock surprise.

She poked me on the arm with her elbow—her way of giving a love pat. "You know what I mean, Max. Don't forget, I can read your mind."

"Ooh, that's dangerous."

"Don't flatter yourself, big boy. Figuring out guys is as simple as playing with a puppy. Guys think about sex from the moment they open their eyes in the morning. And if it's not about sex, it's about sports. Politics, religion, the environment, and saving the world aren't even on the list. Getting laid, that's all you think about."

"Debra, you make guys sound like we're always rutting," I chuckled.

She smiled. "Want to know how I learned that?"

"Sure."

"I had three older brothers. I'd sneak into the basement when they and their friends were watching TV. They'd have on a football or basketball game, and I'd hide behind a sofa and listen to them brag about how they were going to get their girlfriends to have sex. They were like little goats, all horny and feisty, wanting to get into the corral with the young females. Teenage boys . . . horny goats . . . same species. I got an early education."

I roared. "Deb, you're a ballbuster."

"Not really. I like guys. I get along better with them than I do girls, in case you hadn't noticed."

"Yeah, I see you with jocks a lot. Do you ever date them?"

As soon as I said it, I felt I'd pried into Debra's personal life. If she were gay, I didn't want to hear any more.

"I love talking about sports, but jocks are pretty one-dimensional. I'm dating a cool guy who's an art student. He's been to Paris, Rome, and Amsterdam and wants to move to Europe when he graduates in June. I might go over with him next summer. We have great conversations about art, music, books—not what I'd get if I dated a jock."

"Interesting. I didn't know about that," I said.

She shrugged. "No reason you should. We don't mix in the same social circles, just in class. You have more depth than most of the other jocks. I like that about you."

"I like your spunk, Debra. No one's going to walk over you."

She smiled in a coy way that made her more appealing. There was a female under all that Chicago sportswear.

"You're right. There's a ditch outside town where you'll find a couple of guys who thought they could take advantage of me. Take my word; they're pretty bloody and bruised."

I roared again, loving her sass. "I'll bet they are, Deb. I wouldn't want to get on your bad side."

"Hey, we're not here to talk about me. I want to know what you're going to do about the tip I gave you about Amanda. It's a good one; she'll be impressed."

"I'm going to see her play."

"Good. Let me know what you think of it." She got up from the table, pointed a finger at me, and made a clicking sound, like cocking a pistol. "Remember, hot stuff: Tickets for your first game in the majors."

"Got it."

"See you Wednesday morning."

* * *

Tika and I went to *His Girl Friday* on Saturday night. It was a hilarious romp with actors running around a stage set up in the round. The play was about a newspaper editor who uses every trick in the book to keep his ace reporter ex-wife from remarrying.

Amanda was a terrific comedienne, delivering her lines like a pro. She had the audience in stitches. I howled at her hilarious riffs and punch lines. Her timing was amazing.

Amanda wore a 1930s-style long dress that clung to her sleek body like skin. I couldn't take my eyes off her thighs and firm buttocks as she strolled across the stage like she owned it. Every time she passed close to our second-row seats, I felt my blood pressure rising. By the third act, I was sitting on my hands to keep from reaching out to touch her.

Tika also enjoyed the play, punching my arm at the risqué dialogue. On the way out, she commented, "Amanda is really good, isn't she, Max? I've seen her on campus but didn't know she was an actress. She's talented, don't you think?"

"She is. She could make it in the movies if she gets a few breaks."

* * *

By the time basketball season began in December, Amanda and I were sleeping together. Saturday nights we stayed at the apartment of a teammate who slept at his girlfriend's place. I was living in the athletic dorm and Amanda in her sorority house, neither private enough to have an affair.

We kept our relationship secret for the first couple of weeks, not wanting to embarrass Tika and Karl. If it was just a sex thing, we'd get it out of our systems and go back to Karl and Tika. But we couldn't get enough of each other. We'd sneak off to the library for a squeeze among the stacks. A couple of times we got caught by students who turned a corner, spotted us, and hurried off, more embarrassed than we were.

At basketball games, Amanda sat behind the team bench, cheering her six-foot-four power forward, who she said was as dumb as a newborn calf. Hung and horny. A sweet guy whom she didn't want to hurt. She decided to ease her way out of the relationship, telling him she needed to spend more time on her studies.

Karl was hurt, of course, and told her, "Yeah, yeah, Amanda, I understand. We'll get back together after basketball season. I'm kinda hoping this is going to be my big year, making the NCAA tourney and being on national TV, even ESPN. Wouldn't that be great! I really want to make it to the NBA, been my dream since I was a kid. Just let me know if, you know, you want to have a little fun some night, you know?"

Then he had winked at her, but Amanda said it looked more like a bug had flown into his eye. She had to bite her lip to keep from laughing. Nice guy, everyone said about Karl, but "dumb as an ox."

After Christmas break, I arranged for Tika to meet "Nuke," who'd snorted and pawed the ground like a bull whenever he saw us together. I had him drive her back to her sorority house one night when my truck wouldn't start. (I'd removed a spark plug wire and put it back after they'd left the party.)

A month later, at semester break, I handed Tika off to Nuke. Tika wasn't too upset; Nuke had a new Audi and was a flashy dresser and a great dancer. He spoiled her with flowers and love poems copied from Rod McKuen.

When baseball season started in March, Amanda was in the stands at every game. I was hitting the ball like never before, flying around the bases and scooping up ground balls like my glove was a vacuum cleaner.

Amanda cheered when I came to bat or flipped a ground ball

to first base. I was born to play second base, with lightning reactions and a strong throwing arm. I wanted to play baseball forever.

"I can't take my eyes off you when you're out there, Max," Amanda said when we won the North Central Intercollegiate Athletic Conference, beating UND like we had in football. "You move across the infield like a ballet dancer, so smooth, making every play look easy."

Major league scouts were in the stands during the NCIAC tournament, as well as the NCAA northern regionals, which we also won, advancing to the College World Series in Omaha in June. They'd made courtesy calls to my coach to let him know they were scouting me for the upcoming major league draft.

He'd told them I had the tools to make it in the majors and played best against the strongest teams. He'd watched me mature during the previous three years. He sent them my stats: my batting average, base-running speed, and defensive record. Every season I ran faster, hit better, and turned more double plays. Being chosen team captain by my teammates was a big plus, something the scouts thought was promising.

I was lucky to have a hitting streak during the NCAIC tournament and northern regionals, hitting .410, driving in at least one run per game, and smacking four home runs in ten games.

I was thrilled when the Boston Red Sox drafted me in the second round. I was going to play in the majors! But I had little time to celebrate, because NDSU was headed to Omaha. I was on top of the world.

3
———————

The College World Series is a major sporting event at the level of the NCAA Final Four, the Super Bowl, and the World Series. The eight best college baseball teams go to Omaha to battle for the national championship. It was the first time in history that NDSU or any team in our conference had advanced so far.

When we arrived, Omaha was festooned with banners promoting the CWS all over the city, at the airport, on billboards into town, in hotels, and in parks.

It was an honor to be at the CWS, playing in a state-of-the-art stadium in front of 24,000 fans, the largest crowd I'd played before. As I was taking fielding practice before the first game, I scanned the crowd that had come to Omaha to watch future major leaguers even though we were almost unknown outside of our campuses.

The playing field was impressively manicured, with neat white chalk foul lines, a stunningly green outfield, and a perfectly groomed infield. The dugouts and locker rooms were the cleanest and most modern I'd ever seen.

I was determined to play the best baseball of my young career.

My parents were in the stands with Amanda. Dad was the sheriff in Williams County in the far western part of the state; Mom was a high school English teacher. They had been my biggest fans through Little League, high school baseball, and my college career.

The three of them were seated behind our dugout, and they cheered when I ran out of the dugout onto the field for our first game. Amanda whooped like a cowboy while Dad clapped and yelled, "You go, Max! Do your best!"

When I returned to the dugout between innings, Amanda and Dad were talking and laughing as they waved at me. I sneaked a look back when I was in the on-deck circle waiting to bat and saw her teasing Dad or telling a joke. He laughed, tipped back his head, and roared.

I hit a double in the ninth inning, scoring the runner from second, breaking the tie, for our first victory in the CWS. Our team high-fived on the field, and when we trotted back to the dugout, Amanda and Dad were getting along like old friends, sharing a bag of popcorn, his arm behind her seat. Amanda was pointing to my teammates, probably filling him in on where they were from, their girlfriends, and what they were studying. She was charming him, and he was soaking up the attention.

Mom was more sedate, waving every time I returned to our dugout. She looked proud to be in the stadium. I loved my mom; she'd helped me through rough patches in my teenage years when I'd had a wild streak.

Competition at the CWS was fierce, as you'd expect, as the best college teams in the country were playing. We got a few breaks, our pitching staff was superb, and we won four straight games to advance to the winner's bracket.

Before games, I had a taste of what it would be like when I

reached the major leagues. I signed autographs in the CWS program as high school boys and their dads congratulated me on signing with the Red Sox. I was interviewed by sportswriters and broadcasters who complimented me about how well I was playing.

We met Louisiana State in the championship series, best two games out of three. We won the first game, then lost the next two. The last was a heartbreaker of 8-7 in extra innings.

In the last championship game, I hit a home run and a double, walked twice, scored three times, and stole two bases. When our center fielder slugger struck out to end the game, I was stranded at third, just ninety feet away from tying the game. It was sad to watch the Louisiana State team swarm toward the pitcher's mound to hoist the winning pitcher on their shoulders. I watched in silence and walked slowly toward our dugout, where my teammates, stone-faced, watched the on-field celebration that could have been ours if the ball had bounced our way a couple of times in the ninth inning. That's baseball; you win some and you lose some. It's hardest to lose the biggest games.

But my consolation was that my baseball career wasn't over that summer. I was moving on to the major leagues. I finished the series with a .401 batting average and was named Most Valuable Player of the CWS. I was thrilled, even though we didn't take home the championship trophy.

After the final game, I joined Amanda, Mom, and Dad for dinner at an Omaha Steakhouse. I was exhausted from the series, having played almost every day for two weeks. But I was also exhilarated to be with the people I loved the most.

"We're all proud of you, son," Dad said, beaming at me. His voice was hoarse after two weeks of cheering in the stands.

He reached over and squeezed Amanda's hand. "And we enjoyed having Amanda with us. She's your biggest fan, next to us, of course."

Amanda's face was sunburned from long afternoon games in

the stands. She looked tired after taking final exams and then immediately flying to Omaha for the series. "I loved coming to Omaha, even though we didn't win," she said, a hint of fatigue in her voice. "I was lucky my professors let me take finals early so I could be here. I wouldn't have missed this for the world. Wasn't it fun?"

"It sure was, dear," Mom said. She was also sunburned and tired from two weeks away from home. Mom was a homebody; she loved being in her garden or volunteering at Mercy Hospital in the summer.

We ate prime rib and baked potatoes and talked about how we needed to wind down and relax after the stress of the series. Amanda would be joining us at home for a visit before going to see her mother.

Amanda said, "Did Max tell you that the first time we met, he charmed me by talking about baseball like a philosopher? I was mesmerized. Something clicked. I knew we'd end up together. Remember, Max?"

She and I had joked about that October night, but I was surprised that she would tell my parents. "I'll never forget, sweetheart. It was a chilly October night after we beat UND. We drank beer and celebrated in a corral with a huge bonfire."

"It must have been fun," Mom said to Amanda. "I met Max's dad at NDSU also. We went to keg parties too after big football games. Were you on a date?"

"Oh, no," Amanda said, reaching over and squeezing my hand. "We were with other people. A friend of Max's introduced us."

"Oh! Tell me more," Mom said, watching me squirm. "Who were you with, Max?"

Amanda jumped in. "Oh, Max was with a freshman girl, but a mutual friend, Debra, introduced us. She had a crush on Max from marketing class."

"Nah," I said, "she didn't have a crush on me; she likes all jocks. Debra knows more about sports than most guys. Just a friend, nothing else."

Amanda said, "Deb's a character, a little wacky but funny and popular. Everyone on campus knows her."

"Tell me more about your drama classes, Amanda," Mom said, changing the subject.

"Ooh, my second-favorite topic," Amanda said, her eyes lighting up like Christmas candles. "I love acting and old movies. Do you like movies?"

"Since I was a little girl," Mom said. "We had two theaters in my hometown. I went every week. My favorite actors were Doris Day, Jimmy Stewart, Grace Kelly, and Cary Grant. Way before your time, but I loved those old romantic comedies."

"They're classics from the fifties and sixties," Amanda said. "We watched them in my History of Cinema class. My favorite actress of that era was Audrey Hepburn."

"Oh, I love Audrey Hepburn's movies!" Mom said, her eyes lighting up. "Especially *Breakfast at Tiffany's*."

"Such a sweet story, wasn't it?" Amanda said. "Her costar was George Peppard. My favorite Hepburn movies are *Charade*, with Cary Grant, and *Roman Holiday*, with Gregory Peck. She was so young but was cast with leading male actors."

"Who knows, Amanda," Mom said. "Maybe you'll be in a movie one day."

Amanda smiled at Mom, her pink cheeks glowing from her sunburn. "So nice of you to say that. Thank you, Mrs. Bauer. That would be a dream!"

"Please call me Marian, dear."

* * *

manda and I flew back to my hometown, Williston, after the CWS. We wanted a few quiet days before I would fly to Boston to begin my baseball career and Amanda would go home to spend time with her mother.

Mom and Dad were in their routine. Dad, as Williams Country sheriff, went to work at the courthouse, and Mom worked in her garden and had coffee with her friends. Amanda and I slept late—Mom had her stay in a guest bedroom.

I took Amanda around for a tour of my hometown. We drove past Williston High School and Cutting Field, where I had played football, and the Ardean Aafedt baseball stadium. We went down Main Street from Harmon Park, past the First Lutheran Church that my family attended. We drove past the downtown retail stores to the train station at South Main, and on to the James Memorial Library, one of my favorite places in town.

One afternoon we had burgers and milkshakes at Keenan's drive-in on the outskirts of Williston, where students hung out after school and at night. Then we drove west on Highway 2, past wheat farms and ranches, to the State Line, a nightclub and steakhouse on the border of Montana, where there were rodeos in the summer. Returning to Williston, I drove south to the Missouri River flats, where teenagers parked and steamed up the windows. Rough patches in my teenage years had been because of episodes when I'd returned home late on weekends, mussed up after late nights at the flats. Mom knew what was going on. Moms usually do.

Wherever we drove around town, people recognized Dad's car and waved to me. It felt great, returning home and being remembered. "You're a hometown hero, Max," Amanda said. "Your mom showed me some Williston Herald articles from when you played at Omaha. You were on the front page every day."

"It's a small town, honey. It doesn't take much to make the front page. Yesterday's lead story was about some cattle that broke a fence north of town and got out on the highway. The highway patrol had to stop traffic so the rancher could round them up. That's news in a rural county."

Amanda flew home after four days to see her mother before joining me in Pawtucket, Rhode Island, where I started playing with the Red Sox minor league team.

The day before I left for the East Coast, Dad and I went for a drive, a familiar route we'd taken often when I was growing up. Four miles west of Williston, he turned south onto Highway 85, crossing the Lewis and Clark Bridge over the Missouri River and driving into the rich bottomlands of wheat farms and small ranches. Dad drove up to the flat, grassy prairies of Indian Hills and turned west onto an asphalt road that turned to gravel. We passed fields of durum wheat, barley, and sunflowers that had been planted in May. It felt good to be driving in prairies and farm country, seeing songbirds perched on fence posts and farmers cutting their first alfalfa of the season. I rolled down the window to feel the warm summer air flowing over my arm.

When Dad stopped the car so I could unlock a cattle fence, I spooked a flock of pheasants hiding in a nearby wheat field. Three colorful roosters and six hens rose with a raucous burst that startled me. They flew low over the wheat field, the rooster's long tail feathers looking like something from a Chinese scarf, then fluttered down a quarter of a mile away in stalks of golden wheat.

"Be nice to come hunting here in the fall," I said to my dad when I got back in the car.

"We had a mild winter," he said. "Lots of chicks born this spring, so it'll be a good hunting season. I hope you can make it back."

Dad grew quieter the farther we drove. He parked on a bluff

overlooking the lush Missouri River bottomlands, which were the best farm and ranch lands in Williams County. Lewis and Clark had canoed along the Missouri River in the spring of 1804 after spending the winter with the Mandan Indians near the state capital of Bismarck.

We'd parked there many times before to enjoy looking at the farms and ranches a couple of miles from historic Fort Union, at the junction of the Yellowstone and Missouri Rivers and the Montana border. Our ancestors had settled in the Missouri bottomlands more than a hundred years earlier.

Dad was staring at a ranch below us that had all the signs of a prosperous operation: a freshly painted ranch house with a Toyota 4Runner, a Jeep Grand Cherokee, and a Ford Explorer parked in the driveway.

Between the ranch house and the barn was a fenced garden where a woman and a child were watering tomato plants, potatoes, beans, and lettuce. A new John Deere tractor and Case cultivator were parked on an asphalt apron in front of the barn.

Roads around the ranch were free of potholes, and the weeds had been mowed. Everything looked well cared for. All the debris that comes with a large ranching operation—brush and yard waste, garbage, compost, and used machinery parts—was separated and fenced off beside the barn.

We sat quietly, our eyes sweeping east and west at farms and ranches that stretched along the lush river valley. "The old place looks pretty good," Dad said, a bittersweet tone in his voice.

"It sure does, Dad. Most beautiful ranch in the county."

Dad ran a hand over the steering wheel, lost in memories about his family's history in the river valley.

"Grandpa Otto sure hated to lose the farm," he said. Dad's great-grandfather Raymond had settled in the valley in 1902 after moving his family from Wisconsin to homestead six hundred acres given to farmers to cultivate and eventually own.

The family had worked hard, growing wheat, raising dairy cattle, and accumulating almost a thousand acres.

Raymond's son, my dad's Grandpa Otto, took over the farm when Raymond died in 1928. The family's good fortune turned into misfortune when the 1929 Wall Street crash, the Great Depression, and the dustbowl wiped out Otto and thousands of other family farmers across the Great Plains.

"Imagine," Dad said, his voice low. "That ranch could have been ours but for the damned Depression and a decade of disastrous weather. I wasn't alive but heard about it almost every night at the dinner table."

Dad relived our family's bad luck every time we took our drive in the country. He liked being sheriff, but in his heart, he had wanted to be a rancher like his grandfather and father.

We lived on the west side of Williston, where Mom had her garden and Dad tinkered in his shop, repairing a lawnmower, hedge trimmer, tiller, or the old Massey Ferguson tractor Otto had had on the homestead. After Otto lost the farm, he moved the family into town, became a small-town cop, and worked his way up to county sheriff, a position he held until he died the year before I was born.

Dad had followed in his father's footsteps. After getting his degree at NDSU and serving a tour of duty with the Army infantry in Vietnam, he had returned home and worked as salesman for the John Deere implement dealer. But it was a boring job, and he eventually joined the police department. When he was thirty-five years old, he was elected sheriff.

I was proud of my dad. He was respected for his integrity and courage. When I was growing up, he would share stories of solving local crimes, mostly cattle rustling, car thefts, arson, and occasional shootings. I was enthralled, listening to him talk about investigating crimes, questioning witnesses, arresting suspects, and testifying against them in court. I became a devoted reader of mystery and crime novels, passing them along to Dad, who usually dismissed them as simplistic.

"How are things in town, Dad?"

He blinked; my question probably broke his chain of thought about old family stories.

He shrugged and made a sour face. "Things aren't like when you were living here," he said slowly. "We've got a crime wave, with all these damn meth labs. Guys are cooking up crank in abandoned buildings in the country and selling it at truck stops and in dive bars. That stuff's poison—rots your teeth, makes your face look like it's been through a wood chipper. The jail's full of these jerks. They break into homes and steal cars to buy that crap. Meth's a cancer all over the Midwest."

"It's even around campus," I said. "It's a tragedy, messing people up."

"Don't let your friends get on that stuff; it's poison."

"Don't worry, Dad. Nobody I know would touch it."

"That's good. You did the right thing, getting a good education. You think a baseball career's a free pass for the rest of your life, but you'll have to get a job one day when it's over."

"Don't worry, Dad. I've already talked it over with coach and a couple of professors. I'll pick up courses part-time after the season's over until I get my degree. I might even try grad school down the road, maybe get a business or finance degree. I'd like to work for a high-tech or finance company."

"Get your education while you're young. After you start a career, get married, and have kids, there's no time for schooling. And in case you didn't know, your mom and I want grandchildren. Don't make us wait too long. " He turned to me and smiled for the first time since we'd taken the drive.

I blushed. "Dad, I'm only twenty-one. Marriage is a ways off."

"Don't make Amanda wait too long if you're serious about her. She'd make a good wife and mother. Smart—got a good head on her shoulders. And she's crazy about you. Don't mess this up."

My blush deepened. "She is, we might get married, but not right away."

"Your mom and I like her. She'd fit in."

* * *

The Red Sox gave me a signing bonus of $1.5 million. I was on top of the world: a millionaire at twenty-one, in love with the most beautiful coed on campus, and headed to the major leagues.

Amanda and I celebrated by flying to Boston to sign my contract. During the signing ceremony, I wore a Red Sox home jersey and ball cap. After Boston, we flew to New York and went to plays that Amanda had wanted to see. One of the plays had won a Tony as best drama the previous season. The other was an off-Broadway raucous comedy with partial nudity.

Amanda's dream was to act in the theater and maybe be in a movie someday. I encouraged her to follow her dreams, thinking I would be proud to have an actress as my wife.

We ate dinner at The Plaza hotel the night before I was to join my minor league team. We drank champagne and California wines through a four-course dinner. We were both giddy about the exciting future ahead of us.

"I can see it, Max," Amanda said, almost breathless in her excitement. "The Red Sox are playing in Yankee Stadium. I'm in a Broadway play, and both of our names are in lights!" She raised her hands and opened and closed her fists in motions that were like explosions. "We'd be the most glamorous couple in America!"

She looked terrific in a sexy strapless dress—alive, vibrant, and in love. I was so proud of her and happy for both of us. I stroked her bare back and reached over to kiss her cheek. "The baseball star and his Hollywood wife. Someone might even make a movie about us."

Amanda refilled our champagne glasses, and we raised them in a toast. "To Max and Amanda, the most exciting couple in New York. May we be as happy every day in the future as we are tonight!"

4

I joined the Red Sox organization in July, eager to play professional ball. I had been assigned to the minor league AAA Red Sox in Pawtucket, Rhode Island, an old fishing village scarred by rust-belt recessions.

The transition was challenging. I was playing against rookies like myself, fresh from college; guys with a couple of minor league seasons under their belts; and grizzled veterans who'd bounced up and back from the majors to the minors, trying desperately to make the roster in the major league Red Sox lineup.

Professional baseball is all about fierce competition among position players who are sometimes friends, each trying to scratch out extra hits to bump up his batting average. Coaches are always looking for players who make big plays on both offense and defense: batting in base runners in a close game, making a double play to shut down an opponent's rally, or stealing a base in a clutch situation.

The more consistently you improve your performance, the better your chances at staying in the lineup. And everyone's watching . . . coaches, teammates, and the general manager in Boston.

Amanda followed me to the East Coast, helping me burn through my bonus money. We were like kids at a carnival, jabbering nonstop, joking and teasing, grabbing each other like horny teenagers. We were having a blast.

We couldn't keep our hands off each other. Our sex was nuclear. We were living in a world of unrestrained appetites. It was intoxicating. Neither one of us wanted the summer to end, so we didn't talk about D-day, departure day.

At the end of August, Amanda went back to NDSU. In September I fulfilled a boyhood dream when I got called up to join the Red Sox during a hot American League East race against the Yankees.

After the minor league season, major league teams expand their rosters from twenty-five to forty, calling up promising minor leaguers to see how they perform in the bigs.

When I showed up in the locker room for my first game, I looked around at Red Sox veterans I'd followed on TV and in the sports pages: Mo Vaughn, Wade Boggs, and Roger Clemens. They were demigods to minor leaguers like myself who dreamed that one day we'd be in the dugout with them, picking up tips and learning how to survive in "the bigs."

I played in the third game after I was called up. In my first at bat as a Red Sox player, I singled, stole second, and raced home to score on a double to the Green Monster, Fenway Park's left outfield wall.

I was in heaven—in the record book as a major leaguer at the age of twenty-one. I pinch-hit in late innings in a dozen games that fall. I hit one homer and two doubles but whiffed ten times. Not bad for someone who'd started the baseball season the first week in March, playing six small colleges in Texas when North Dakota was still blanketed in snow. I ended the season six months later in Fenway Park, even if I sat on the bench during that last game.

I was the luckiest man in the world.

I returned to NDSU in October after the Yankees won the division. The dean of the business school let me enroll late in two courses for six credits. At that rate, I could finish my degree in four more years, fulfilling my parents' wishes and my own.

When I wasn't in class or studying, I worked out in the weight room with the football team and ran sprints on the track. I needed to build strength in my upper body and get a step faster on the base path. I kept a low profile on campus, but students recognized me and asked how it was to play in Yankee Stadium. However, I wasn't back at NDSU for glory, but to stay in shape, continue my studies, and get ready for spring training.

Amanda and I lived in an off-campus apartment in University Village. We went to a few parties but spent more time at movies, cooking together, or eating out with former teammates and their dates. She was in rehearsals for the drama classes' production of *Death of a Salesman*, cast as Willy Loman's beleaguered wife. It was not an easy role for a young beauty, wearing tattered dresses and scuffed shoes and having shaggy hair tied up in a scarf. Her makeup made her look like she was a forlorn fifty-year-old wife beaten down by life and Willy's miserable tale.

On opening night, the cast got a standing ovation. The audience cheered when Amanda took her bows, holding the hand of the actor who played Willy. She beamed, waved, and blew kisses to the audience, basking in the applause of two hundred people crammed into the Askanase Theatre, with its low ceiling, threadbare carpeting, and a curtain that looked like it dated back to the Vaudeville era. But for Amanda, it was like being on Broadway.

"You were fabulous, sweetheart!" I gushed as we drove back to our apartment after the performance. She sat close, pressing her body against me.

"I love that role," she said. "Arthur Miller is a genius. It's draining to play someone lost in life, but I felt the part. Serious drama makes me stretch, playing someone beaten down by life, watching her husband slowly dying in front of her eyes. There's so much desperation and raw emotion in *Salesman* . . . resignation to life's sadness, lost hopes, and despair. I don't know where that comes from."

"It's talent," I said. "You're a natural. You can play drama and comedy. Your talent will get you on Broadway one day. It will happen. I know it will."

She reached over again, her fingers caressing the back my neck. "Max, I'm so glad you're encouraging. It means so much that you want me to be an actress." Then she whispered in my ear, "But the role I most want to play is your wife."

* * *

I was walking across the quad one snowy November afternoon when I heard a voice yell, "Hey, Max!"

I turned around and saw a woman tromping through the snow, bundled in a fashionable leather jacket, her arm linked with a younger guy. She ran to me and wrapped her arms around my down ski jacket. "Debra! Great to see you, babe. I never would have recognized you, all bundled up."

"I heard you were back," she squealed, her breath coming out like puffs of cotton candy in the chilly air. "Where you been hiding?"

Debra's Chicago sports jersey and ball cap were gone. She was wearing designer jeans that made her legs look long and thin. Her cute beret was tilted to the side, and a multicolored scarf decorated her neck. Her hair was longer and styled, falling in curls to her shoulders. She looked terrific, even sexy, like a Midwestern snow queen.

"Amanda and I are living in University Village, kinda lying low."

She punched my arm like she used to do in marketing class. "Hey, hot stuff, I saw you play a night game on TV in Yankee Stadium. You looked soooo cool in a Red Sox uniform. You got a double, and I screamed so loud I woke my roommates!" She laughed, a joyful outburst that came out in a gauzy white cloud.

"It was a thrill, playing in the House That Ruth Built. You wouldn't believe how loud it is in Yankee Stadium, with all the seats filled with screaming fans. It gave me goose bumps the first few games."

"I'll bet. I would have loved to have come to see you play in person, but I was already back in school. Is major league pitching as tough as I hear? Those Yankee flamethrowers were smoking 'em at you."

"Yeah, it's a different game, Deb, but I'm learning. Hey, how are you doing? You look terrific." I patted her arms like packing snow on a snowman.

She flicked a wisp of hair from her eyes with a gloved hand. Her cheeks were flushed from the cold, and her eyes were sparkling like sunlight shining on a frozen lake. "Couldn't be better," she said, looking over at her boyfriend. "Max, this is Chet, my new guy," she said, nudging him. He was a couple of inches shorter than Debra and wore horn-rimmed glasses. "He's a poly-sci major, going to law school next year. Just what the world needs, another lawyer, right? But I cut him slack. He says he wants to be a senator one day."

"Nice to meet you, Max," Chet said, reaching out a gloved hand. "Deb talks about you all the time. You're her favorite ballplayer. I love baseball and made it to most of your games this spring. And way to go at the College World Series! You were terrific, even MVP!"

"Thanks," I mumbled, uneasy with flattery from people I didn't know. "You're lucky to be hanging out with Debra. She's a great lady. She's got more brains than most professors."

"Oh! Oh!" Debra squealed, bouncing up and down in the

snow. "Guess what, Max! Great news! I interviewed with corporate recruiters last month. Procter & Gamble is flying me to Cincinnati to interview for a sales program in New York. How about that! If I get the job, I'll be working in the Big Apple." She punched my arm again, this time harder.

"Congratulations, Deb. That's great! I'm happy for you."

"I'm so excited!" she bubbled, stomping her feet in the snow. "I can finally leave the windswept prairies, snow drifts, and blizzards of North Dakota and spread my wings. I can go to the Guggenheim, run in Central Park, ride to the top of the World Trade Center, and prowl around Greenwich Village on weekends."

"Good for you. Life gets more exciting when you leave North Dakota."

She wrinkled her brow like she was puzzled by something. "So, Max, what are you doing back on campus? Just hanging around?"

"I'm taking a couple of classes. Working out, staying in shape for spring training."

"From what I hear, you and Amanda are pretty tight. Glad that's working out for both of you."

"She's doing well. She was in *Death of a Salesman.*"

"Oh, yeah. I saw it last week. She's really good. You must be proud of her."

"Sure am."

She held up her hand, waving with her gloved fingers. "Hey, Chet and I gotta run to class. Call me sometime. Let's grab a beer like the old days."

"Sure thing, Deb."

She stood on her toes and planted a kiss on my cheek, "See you, hot stuff. Don't forget old Deb, your biggest fan! And remember, you owe me tickets to see you play at Fenway. Don't forget our little deal last fall about . . . you know what."

"Yes, I remember." I smiled. "It was a good tip. I'll let you know when I get called up next season."

"Deal!" she shouted. She held up her gloved hand, and we high-fived.

I watched her hurry off through the snow, her arm linked with Chet's like she was dragging him off to her cave. I didn't ask what had happened to the boyfriend she was going to visit in Europe. She didn't seem to be having trouble collecting boyfriends, and none of them were going to walk over Deb. Good for her.

I didn't call her, although maybe I should have. I didn't want to make Chet jealous as we rattled on about "old times" and traded sports trash.

Amanda and I went to a couple of fraternity parties, but I felt out of place. New pledges had joined the fraternity, and I had little in common with green eighteen-year-old freshmen who seemed overwhelmed with their first semester in college. I spent time with my old teammates and worked on getting in shape for the next season.

I was counting the days until spring training, hoping to make the team and play at Fenway Park, Yankee Stadium, and Comiskey Park. The next summer was going to be thrilling.

5

I arrived at spring training in Vero Beach, Florida, in February, eight pounds heavier, in great shape, and swinging a hot bat. But I might have worked out too hard over the winter; I felt a twinge in my left shoulder that slightly hindered my swing. Instead of whipping the bat around level, I rolled it over when I made contact. Instead of hitting line drives to the outfield, I squibbed dribblers to the infield. Our batting coach worked with me, videotaping me and helping me adjust my swing.

When I returned to Pawtucket in May, I got off to a slow start. A month into the season, my batting average had dropped fifty points from my rookie year.

Amanda's mother, Olive, didn't like to travel and had visited Amanda only once at NDSU after we started dating. I saw Olive again at Amanda's graduation in June, but we still had nothing more than polite conversation. Amanda's aunt, her deceased father's sister, showed up as well, and we got along better.

Amanda and I were married in her Wisconsin hometown in July, but I had only a long weekend, as baseball season was in full swing. I sat between Amanda and her mother at the rehearsal dinner. Olive spent most of her time pointing out her friends seated nearby, telling me about their families, jobs, hobbies, and grandchildren.

Olive didn't have any interest in baseball. She and Mom talked at our reception while Dad was joking around with my former NDSU teammates who'd flown in for the weekend.

"Olive doesn't open up much about herself, does she?" Mom remarked to me at breakfast on Sunday morning before we flew back East. "I tried to get to know her but didn't have much luck. I don't think she's a happy woman. Amanda's father died when he was in his thirties, and Olive remarried and divorced twice. She seems sad to me. I invited her to visit this summer, but she was evasive. I doubt she'll come."

We postponed our honeymoon until baseball season was over. Amanda interviewed with local theaters but was hired by an agency to work in Boston as a hostess at corporate conventions. Between events, she interviewed at TV stations and landed small roles in local commercials.

Playing in the minors meant taking buses to places like Buffalo, Syracuse, and Lehigh Valley; staying at Holiday Inns; and eating at franchise steakhouses. My teammates were also former college players, as well as veterans who had bounced up and down from the minors to the majors, getting older as they watched younger, stronger, and faster players show up every season.

My roommate on the road was Arnie Swinburne, a Minnesota farm boy who was twenty-eight years old and a weary minor league veteran. Our brief baseball careers were similar. Like me, he'd signed a contract after playing three years at the University of Minnesota. He'd been plagued by wrist and shoulder injuries and a torn knee ligament that had required multiple surgeries. His brief appearances in the majors had been disastrous; the first time he was called up, he went two for twenty-eight. The second time he struck out eight times in three games. He hadn't been called up a third time.

"It gets tougher every year, Max," Arnie told me as we were sipping beers in our motel room after losing a game in Rochester in which he'd pinched-hit and struck out in the ninth inning. "I had big dreams. I was twenty-one years old when I signed with a bonus that was more money than I thought I'd make in my life. But, man, things just didn't turn out the way I'd hoped."

"I'm sorry, Arnie. We all get bad breaks."

"But it's not only my baseball career. My home life's a mess, too. My wife's having our third baby in September. It's tough on her, popping out three kids one right after another, bing-bang-boom. She's moving home so her mother can help with the kids. She's always on my back . . . says I'm crazy to be playing ball when I should have a real job and come home at night like other guys."

Arnie sounded like a miserable old fart drinking with buddies in a dive bar, swapping life stories of woe, bad luck, and hard times.

"But you're young. You've still got potential," I said, trying to cheer him up. "You can still bounce back this season."

Arnie shook his head, worry lines deepening around his mouth and eyes. "Thanks for the boost, Max, but I'm not so sure," he said, draining his beer and tossing the can into the wastebasket. "It's not just my hitting. I worry about everything." He stretched out the word everything with the pain of somebody who's given up. "My confidence is in the crapper. I get up to bat, worried that I'll strike out or hit a feeble grounder. I never had doubts when I was younger. I swung for the fences every pitch. I struck out a lot but had my share of extra bases and home runs. I haven't had a hitting streak since last season. Coach is working with me, but how can you teach someone confidence at the plate?"

"Yeah, I know what you mean," I said, trying to sound

encouraging, although it's hard when someone is wallowing in self-pity, expressing all doubt and little hope. I never wanted to be like that. "Sometimes things just pile on, Arnie. But you can beat it. Don't get too down on yourself."

"I just don't, you know, think I can make it anymore in baseball," he said, opening his fourth beer. "I got too many worries. You young guys are motivated, having the time of your lives, cocky. You'll make it to the show. I don't even think about making it anymore. I think I'm done with baseball."

"Don't give up, Arnie. We've still got a month left in the season."

But Arnie was finished; it was written all over his face.

* * *

By August, I was in the groove, hitting .340, getting extra base hits, and scoring a run or two every game. Coaches like to see a player make a difference every game.

I got called up to the majors in August and again in September. Boston wasn't in a race for the playoffs, so management was calling up younger players to let them get playing time when games didn't count. I called Debra to offer tickets, but she begged off with a busy work and travel schedule.

"Max, you wouldn't believe it. P&G put me on a team with huge hotel accounts—the Hilton, Radisson, and Holiday Inn. I'm meeting corporate big shots and playing golf with them at fancy country clubs in Connecticut and New Jersey. I'm having a blast. But I swear, next season I'm going to carve out a few days and come to see you play. I don't miss a game when you're on TV. Hit one deep for old Deb!"

* * *

I played in twenty-five games, batted .298, and hit two home runs and six RBIs—not bad for a second year. I was thrilled to wear a Red Sox uniform again, all crispy white with red lettering when we played at Fenway.

My season was over by the end of September. I decided not to return to NDSU to take classes. Amanda was getting steady work and wanted to stay on the East Coast. We rented an apartment in Boston for the winter and flew home to see my parents at Thanksgiving.

We relaxed for a few days. Amanda and I took walks around Williston, which had already had blizzards. Snow blanketed everything—pretty, but it was hard to drive on the icy roads. Amanda helped Mom bake a turkey dinner and pumpkin pies. We had cousins, aunts, and uncles around the dinner table, as well as friends of Mom and Dad's who didn't have family in the area.

On the Saturday after Thanksgiving, Dad and I drove out to the old homestead. He'd been preoccupied during the holiday, and I knew something was on his mind. We mostly talked about baseball and the next season, when I'd be back for my third year.

"Something I should tell you before you leave, Max. Remember Bud Hollings?"

"Sure. I went to school with Ronny. I think he's living in Chicago. And their daughter, Katrina—she's younger."

He nodded. "That's right. Nice family. Been a good influence in town. Bud's the county treasurer."

"I remember."

He made a sucking noise and nervously tapped the steering wheel, a habit when something was bothering him.

He sighed, then swore—something he didn't do unless he was upset. "Bud's been embezzling from the county."

"What? Oh, no. That's terrible."

"Yup. He built a new home a couple of years ago on University Drive. He and Carol have been taking vacations to Florida and California every winter. I used to golf with him. We were on the church board together. I knew he had rich relatives in Seattle, and I thought that was where he was getting the money for the new home and vacations. Turned out he wasn't. So I'm arresting him Monday morning. The DA's got a list of charges for an indictment. The news is going to shake up people in town. It'll be a real mess."

"That's terrible, Dad. I'm sorry to hear this. That poor family. I could tell something was on your mind."

"I don't hide things well. I feel terrible, one of my best friends is a crook." He slammed a fist on the steering wheel.

"I know you liked Bud. What a shame. This'll ruin his family."

"Sure will. I used to think I had a good sense about people. But I didn't see this coming. You think you know someone and trust them. That's my business. Then something like this happens, and you question your judgment. When you're sheriff, you learn psychology pretty fast. Spend five minutes with someone, and you know if they're a liar or if they cheat on their wife or their taxes. I never thought I'd be so wrong about someone I'd known for years."

"It's not your fault, Dad. He fooled a lot of people."

"Your mom's shook up too. She and Carol play bridge and help out at church. Mom was with her a couple of weeks ago and said Carol seemed different. All quiet and not talking much. Bud knows what's coming. Don't see him in town anymore; he stays home. I hate to be the one to arrest him, but it's my job."

"I'm sorry, Dad," I said, watching him stare out the window. He'd aged since the last time I'd been home. Lines creased his face, and liver spots were showing on his hands.

"You meet mostly losers, whiners, and troublemakers in this job," he continued, his jaw clenched, his eyes staring into the distance. He was in real pain. "You know when someone's lying to you or hiding something. But people who make it through your truth filter, you trust them. Bud was one of those. I was probably the person most shocked when the DA said they were going to indict him. State boys came and audited the county books, and they have evidence he embezzled at least a million dollars from me and every other taxpayer in the county. No different than a guy who robs a bank or a liquor store."

"I'm sorry, Dad."

"I was suckered in just like everyone. He lied to all of us. And I didn't see it. Maybe I should get into another line of work —be a bank teller or a mail carrier." He made a fist and thumped it on the steering wheel again, his jaw tight. I reached over and patted him on the shoulder.

"You'll get through this, Dad. A month from now, it will be behind you. People will look to you to know things will be okay."

"That's what your mother said. You been talking to her?"

"No, she hasn't said a word about it."

He looked over at me, the wrinkles around his eyes looking deeper.

"Your mom and I need a vacation. Okay with you if we come to Florida this winter to watch you play?"

"Yes! Dad, I really want you to come. It will be good for both you and Mom. We'll go deep-sea fishing. Some of the play-ers' dads come down every spring."

"That'd be nice, son. Maybe I'll meet other fellows who don't know what I do. I don't want to talk about work or prob-lems or any of that other stuff. Just have fun."

Amanda and I returned to Boston on Sunday. She was working for an event-planning firm coordinating holiday parties in Boston for major corporations: Raytheon, EMC, Fidelity, and State Street. She'd have good exposure that might help her make contacts to advance her acting career.

I loafed most of the time, reading thriller and detective paperbacks by Michael Connolly, Dennis Lehane, and Alex Berenson. I'd been reading a lot during the season and could get through a book in two or three days. I gobbled them up like M&M's. In the afternoons, I worked out at a gym and took long runs along the Charles River.

Amanda's mother came the week before Christmas. They went shopping every afternoon, and we ate dinners out.

My conversations with Olive were polite and formal, probably typical for a new mother-in-law and son-in-law relationship. I didn't mention anything about baseball. She was more interested in talking about her job at an insurance company, collecting antiques, and playing bridge with her women friends, most of whom were divorced or widowed.

One evening we were watching TV while Amanda was reading a script in our home office.

"I sure hope you and Amanda have a baby soon," Olive said, dropping her little bomb while I was watching the news. "I can't wait until I'm a grandma so I can spoil my grandchildren." Her tone was not particularly joyful; it was more like that of a nurse who was about to give you a shot and was telling you, "This won't hurt."

"All my friends are grandmas," Olive continued, not even looking at me. She was twisting her fingers in her lap, a nervous habit I'd noticed before. "They show me pictures holding their grandbabies, dressing them, and taking them out in strollers. I want to be like them. I'll be fifty-five next February, the right age to hold a grandbaby."

I felt on the spot. Amanda and I hadn't talked much about having kids. We were both involved with our careers and didn't want to change anything.

"It's nice that your friends are enjoying being grandmothers, Olive," I said, feeling like I was tiptoeing through a minefield without a map. "But Amanda and I haven't talked about starting a family yet. We're still young and starting our careers. Amanda is doing great; I don't know if she wants to take time to have a child."

Olive gave me a sour look, like she'd seen a worm floating in her soup. "Oh, well," she said, with a jagged sigh. "I know. I know. I just had to say it. Amanda tells me the same thing. I don't understand young people anymore. You want high-powered jobs and fancy cars and big homes. We weren't so lucky back in the Stone Age, when I was growing up. We married young, had babies, went to church every Sunday, and worked like slaves. I wish I could have had more kids, but I had problems, you know, down there," She pointed at her stomach. "My doctor didn't think I should have any more after Amanda." She stopped twisting her fingers, laid her hands flat on her thighs, and kept them there.

I didn't know how to respond. Olive made me uncomfortable with her grim fustiness. I was relieved that Amanda was so different from her mother, more ambitious and optimistic. She had inherited some of her mother's features: eyes that pulled you in, high cheekbones, and a delicate chin. But Olive was almost gaunt. She dressed like she lived in a nursing home: high-necked, shapeless blouses that barely revealed bumps of breasts. Not like Amanda, fortunately, who had delicious curves and wonderful fullness where it counted.

Amanda had shared with me only superficial details of her family history. She lamented that Olive had had her share of heartaches. Amanda's father had died when Amanda was five years old. Olive had remarried after a year but divorced her second husband when Amanda was ten years old. She had married a third time when Amanda was twelve, but that had ended in divorce as well. Olive had been alone for more than fifteen years by this time. Amanda wasn't in touch with her two stepfathers, and I suspected she hadn't cared for either of them.

The only picture I'd seen of Amanda's father had been taken when she was four years old, sitting on his lap. He had a shock of dark hair combed over his head. He was handsome, with a roguish Peter O'Toole grin that made me think Amanda had inherited some of his traits.

"Mom had terrible luck with men after Dad died," Amanda had shared with me when we were planning our wedding. "I spent summers with my dad's brother and family after Dad died. My uncle's family didn't like the men Mom married. One was lazy and couldn't hold onto a job. The other was a creep. I went to live with my uncle's family in Bismarck when I was fourteen until I went to NDSU."

I felt sad about Amanda's upbringing, although she'd adapted well and didn't seem affected by Olive's troubled marital life.

* * *

Amanda and I took winter vacations, one to Vero Beach to find an apartment for spring training and another to the Bahamas and Virgin Islands, where we laid on the beach, made passionate love every afternoon, swam, and drank daiquiris while watching the sunset from our cabana before dinner. We were living a wonderful life—healthy and in love, with money stashed away for our future.

* * *

By the time I showed up for spring training, I was in good shape, ready for my next season in professional baseball. My dream was to make it in the starting lineup when Boston opened the season on April 2. My third time in the batting cage, I hit under the ball, and it ricocheted off the cage and drilled me in the right shoulder, my throwing arm. I stumbled out of the cage, holding my shoulder like I'd been shot.

X-rays showed that nothing was broken, but I couldn't move my arm without pain. I missed a week of batting practice but ran sprints in the outfield. We had intrasquad games, but my shoulder was too tender to play. A frustrating way to start spring training.

My parents came to spring training, as planned. Dad and I went deep-sea fishing with a few of my teammates and their fathers. He was still preoccupied by Bud's upcoming trial. It turned out Bud had embezzled close to two million dollars from the county.

I felt lucky that I wasn't plagued by the worries I'd heard from Arnie, who hadn't shown up for spring training; from Olive, who hoped a grandchild would get her through loneliness; and from Dad, who'd been betrayed by one of his best friends.

Would I be so fortunate in the years to come?

6

I n the middle of my fourth season, I was called up to the majors in July and again in August to play for the regular second baseman, who had wrenched his knee in a collision at home plate.

I hit .289 in forty games and had four home runs, ten doubles, and twenty RBIs. I was feeling more comfortable playing in the majors; my confidence knew no bounds. In September, we were in a hot pennant race, second in the American League East. We clinched a spot in the playoffs the last weekend of the season, sweeping the Detroit Tigers at their home.

The Red Sox hosted the Anaheim Angels in the first round of the playoffs. But our pitchers were exhausted from the long season, and our two starters couldn't make it past the fourth inning. Our bullpen, weary and beaten up, couldn't keep the Angels from reaching base. We lost the first two games by five and six runs, a disastrous start for a five-game series.

On our charter flight to Los Angeles, I sensed the team had all but given up hope. We were about as likely to win three games to advance to the American League Championship Series as a drunk was to pass up a complimentary happy hour. It wasn't going to happen.

Amanda flew to Los Angeles for the playoffs. She was coming to watch us play and to network with movie industry contacts she'd been referred to by her drama teacher at NDSU and TV producers back East. She had a better week in Los Angeles than I did.

I didn't help the team in LA. I had one hit in two games against the Angels but struck out three times and didn't score. The Sox won the first, but the Angels came back strong in game four. We lost the series, three games to one. I ended the season on the bench, watching the Angels' center fielder catch a long fly ball.

Angels fans cheered like they'd won the World Series. Fireworks exploded over the stadium, and air cannons boomed like Fort Sumter, but there was no joy in our dugout. Our team shuffled through the tunnel to our locker room, cursing our poor showing in the playoffs, grumbling about the ending of a season that had looked so promising during the long summer months of playing when we were number one or number two in our division.

The good news was that Amanda did well in her interviews. An agent arranged screen tests to show to TV producers and independent film directors. The agent was impressed with Amanda and hinted he might be able to get her a small part in an independent movie or a cable show.

We booked a room at a Santa Monica hotel after the series so Amanda could meet the contacts her agent was arranging. While she was at meetings, I walked around the Santa Monica Pier area and had lunch at Thai, Vietnamese, and Italian restaurants. One day I drove along the Pacific Coast Highway to Manhattan Beach, Redondo Beach, Marina del Rey, and Malibu. My previous trips to LA had been for baseball games, and I had never had a chance to experience California more leisurely. I liked visiting but didn't think I could ever live in LA—too much traffic and too many people. A few million too many.

The day before we were to fly home, we were having a relaxing breakfast on our balcony, overlooking the ice-blue Pacific Ocean. We had slept in after a late dinner in Malibu with an agent who wanted to represent Amanda. He had hinted that he could make key introductions to independent film producers who were always looking for new talent.

After our showers, we had put on puffy hotel robes and called room service, which delivered a tray of freshly squeezed orange juice, a pot of coffee, fruit, toast, cereal, and the Los Angeles Times.

The weather in Los Angeles was glorious: fluffy clouds painted against a stunning blue sky. The warm temperatures and fresh air reminded me of boyhood summers when I had worked on a Montana ranch, herding cattle to take them to market. Those had been my best summers until the magical year when NDSU had advanced to the CWS and I had ended the season playing for the Red Sox.

My memories of that Los Angeles morning have never left me. But it was not because of California's beautiful fall weather or my mourning our loss to the Angels. It was the morning Amanda and I had The Conversation.

I was sipping coffee, reading the sports page about the Angels playing the Chicago White Sox for the American League title. Amanda was deeply absorbed in a front-page story in the local news section. As she read, her jaw clenched and her fists clutched the newspaper like she wanted to rip it into shreds. I was puzzled by the tension she was exhibiting but didn't interrupt her. I returned to the sports page until Amanda crumpled the paper.

"Max!" she said, more of a command than a request.

She raised her sunglasses to look at me, her eyes blazing with fury.

"Yes, dear?"

"Put down the sports page. I want to talk." Another command. Not her style.

I did as she said. She stared at me with a look I'd never seen before. I felt chastened, as if she'd caught me reading a porn magazine instead of the sports page. What was going on?

"What is it?" I asked, uneasy about her tone. I sipped my coffee, which suddenly seemed cold.

"Do you think you'd kill someone if you thought it was justified?"

Whoa. This wasn't coming from left field; it was coming from someplace dark and sinister.

"Aaah," I stammered, "wh—what do you mean? I don't understand."

"I said," she emphasized, "would you kill someone if you thought it was justified?" She leaned toward me over the table, her arm brushing her coffee cup and spilling some near her elbow, which she ignored. Her voice was chilly, like wind blowing across a frozen lake.

"What in the world are you talking about, Amanda?"

"Just what I said," she replied, tossing the crumpled paper to me. "Here. Read this."

She pointed to a headline about a Torrance teenager who had stabbed her stepfather during a family argument. I read quickly through the story, turning to an inside page to finish the article. Police had responded to a 911 call about a domestic dispute that had escalated into a stabbing. A photo showed police cars and ambulances at a modest suburban home, emergency lights illuminating gawking neighbors who watched as the EMT team wheeled a gurney out of the house.

The man had died at the hospital the next morning. Police were questioning the mother and daughter and considering filing charges for manslaughter or second-degree murder.

"Tragic story," I said, putting down the paper. "Bad things

happen, unfortunately. A domestic incident gets out of hand, and somebody gets hurt or dies. I'm sorry for them."

Amanda wasn't mollified. "They better not charge her. The daughter was justified to kill her stepfather and protect her mother."

Heavy stuff for a sunny morning in California. I shook my head, not sure how to respond to Amanda's statement.

"It doesn't say she was protecting her mother," I said, trying to sound objective. Amanda had made a definitive judgment about a situation from reading an initial news story. This was quite a departure from her usual pattern of asking questions and wanting to know more before making a decision. "She and her stepfather had an argument about her reckless behavior—taking drugs, hanging out with shady friends," I continued. "It's a sad story, but I don't understand why you're so upset."

"Read between the lines," Amanda said defiantly, her eyes narrowing. "He was abusive and controlling. This wasn't the first time they'd argued. He probably tormented the girl and her mother to show he was 'macho.' I'll bet he molested the poor girl. That's why she was full of rage. He was a bully, a creep, a child molester. He's better off dead!" Her face was flushed, her cheeks on fire as if she herself had been the girl in the story.

I was uncomfortable with Amanda's anger, an emotion I'd rarely seen in her before. Something in the story had enraged her, but I didn't know what it was.

"It doesn't say that, Amanda, only that he and the mother argued a lot. All parents have arguments, probably more when a mother remarries and the stepfather and daughter don't get along. She's a teenager, probably wild and reckless. Their home was a powder keg, the mother in the middle between her husband and daughter, who hated each other. It was ripe for violence. It ended up with him getting killed."

Amanda shook her head. "The mother and daughter can get

on with their lives without him," she said with a scowl, her arms folded across her chest in a gesture of defiance.

"You're making a harsh judgment. Wait until the facts come out. Detectives will investigate, question everyone involved, and get all the background. The district attorney will review the evidence and decide if the daughter should be tried and what the charges will be. Social services will get involved. It could be assigned to juvenile court. There is a legal process."

Amanda wasn't satisfied. "The daughter had the right to kill him," she said coldly. "He was a danger to the family, he wasn't even her father, just some miserable loser her mother married. Extreme measures are called for sometimes."

I shook my head again. "Wait until there's a hearing or trial before you rush to judgment. Why are you so upset?"

She had fire in her eyes. She took a deep breath, leaned back in her chair, picked up a napkin, and wiped up the spilled coffee, dropping the napkin into her half-full coffee cup. She was done with coffee for the morning. She poured half a glass of orange juice from the pitcher, sipped it, and looked at me.

"Sometimes you're naive, Max. You don't know about these things." She put her sunglasses back on and looked out at the ocean. It seemed like she had transported herself a thousand miles away. When she resumed talking, her tone changed from anger to wistfulness, like she was onstage, playing a dramatic scene before an audience. I couldn't decide whether I was listening to my wife or watching a skilled actress playing a role.

"You came from a good family, Max. Your father was a good provider, he was faithful to your mother, they have a solid marriage. You always got what you wanted."

"Yes, I was lucky to have good parents. But what does that have to do with this?"

She took off her sunglasses, uncrossed her arms, and looked at me, her eyes flinty and cold. "Not everybody has the good fortune you had."

"What do you mean?"

She sipped her orange juice, gripping the glass as if she was going to throw it off the balcony. Her face was drained of color, a pale mask of indignation. Her breathing was rapid, the front of her robe rising and falling.

"My stepfather was a creep, just like that guy. I hated him and wished he'd leave."

Actress or wife, she had my complete attention.

"I didn't know. You've never talked about it."

"You know why?" she said icily.

"No, I don't."

"He tried to molest me," she hissed.

New information. I knew that Olive and her second husband had divorced when Amanda was ten years old and that Olive had remarried. That marriage also had ended in divorce when Amanda was living with her uncle and his family.

I had always figured that Olive's brittle shell stemmed from the emotional debris of the early death of Amanda's father and two failed marriages that followed. Amanda had evaded talking about her stepfathers; now I understood why. I remembered what she had said about how she enjoyed playing Willy Loman's beaten down wife in *Death of a Salesman*. Her own upbringing had been in a twisted tale of death, divorce, and two miserable stepfathers, one who had tried to molest her.

"I'm sorry, Amanda. I had no idea."

"There's a lot you don't know," she snapped.

"Then tell me," I said, holding my breath, unsure of what I might hear.

She gazed off toward the ocean again, a sheen of perspiration shining on her forehead. I could sense that she was choosing her words carefully, as if she were tiptoeing through a minefield.

She cleared her throat. "After my father died," she started slowly, "my mother married this rich guy she'd met through work. She was looking for someone who could take care of us financially. Dad didn't have life insurance, and Mom's job didn't pay much, so she let this guy talk her into getting married. He'd been married before. His wife had dumped him—for good reason. He'd ignored his kids, and they were all screwed up."

"I'm sorry. This is the first time you've talked about him. But that can't be why you're so irritated."

She turned to me. "You're right. I never have talked about him. Not much to say, really. They divorced after four years. A couple of years later, she married another rich guy she met through a friend. They only dated a couple of months, and all of a sudden he was living in our house, sleeping in the same bed as my dad had. I didn't like him from the start. I was a teenager and didn't like the way he stared at me—leering like a dirty old man."

Amanda's words were chilling, almost like she was that bitter teenage girl again, afraid and angry, reliving a terrible secret.

"I couldn't be in the same room with him. I'd go to my bedroom and shut the door whenever he came home. Then, when I was thirteen, he came into the bathroom when I was in the shower. I yelled at him to get out. I was so scared. He apologized and said he didn't know I was in there. But he knew what he was doing. The shower was running!"

She took a deep breath before continuing. I was feeling increasingly uneasy, almost afraid to hear what was coming next.

"Not long after that, he came into my bedroom when I was dressing for school. Mom had left for work. I was terrified! I yelled at him and told my mother when she came home. But get this: My mother apologized for him! Said he didn't mean any harm; he was just oblivious sometimes. I was furious with her for not standing up for me, her own daughter!"

I clenched my fists, angry about what had happened. Now I understood why Amanda and Olive weren't close. There had been an invisible wall between them; now I was realizing how that wall had come about. Amanda had been victimized by a creepy stepfather and a mother who wouldn't protect her. A dreadful situation.

Amanda was almost hyperventilating. She wasn't looking at me, but I could see her eyes watering. "Then," she started, as if each word was a hot stone coming out of her mouth, "when I was fourteen, he slid his hand down my shorts when I was in the kitchen getting milk out of the refrigerator. I threw the milk at him, smacked him hard across the face, cursed at him like a pirate, said I'd kick him in the balls if he ever touched me again! I wanted to kill him!"

I was too stunned to speak.

Amanda turned to look at me with tears in her eyes, like a child whose pet had died.

"Now you know why I left home to live with my uncle's family. I never went back to Mom's house until she divorced him. I hope he's dead."

7

———————

I had the best spring training of my career and made the twenty-five-player starting roster my fifth year with the Red Sox. When Boston started the season in Tampa Bay, I pinch-hit in three games, had a hit and a walk, and scored once.

When we opened the season at Fenway, I started the first game on a cold, windy day. We beat the Yankees, our traditional, bad-blood rival.

Through April and May, I played almost every day, rotating with our veteran second baseman, who had back spasms, or pinch-hitting when he was in the lineup. I got on base most games, getting walks, scratching out hits, stealing bases, and scoring. Coaches like to see that you make a difference when you're in the lineup. My teammates congratulated me every time I came into the dugout after scoring, high-fiving and slapping me on the back. "Way to go, Max! This is your year."

My confidence soared; I recalled my conversation with Arnie, whose self-doubt had ended his brief career. I was determined to give the game my best every time I ran onto the field. I upped my mental game with a mantra—Get on base! Run! Score!—which ran through my head when I came to bat.

It worked. By the middle of the summer, I was fourth in the American League in scoring and was named to the All-Star team. Sports magazines said I was going to be one of the next Red Sox greats.

Amanda and I had an apartment in Boston. She was also having a good summer, guest cohosting on an afternoon local entertainment program and working part-time in Boston with the event planning company. She auditioned for a local theater and was cast in a summer stock play. She was happy to be acting again but wasn't pleased with the director and didn't audition for the fall play.

In August, Amanda got a call from her Los Angeles agent to come out to read for a couple of independent movies, which she did. She called me every night to gush about how well she had done in her auditions. She met other young actors, directors, and producers, and they all praised her talent.

In late August, I came home from a long road trip, eager to take a hot shower and fall into bed before Amanda came home that night. But when I opened the door to our apartment, she ran into my arms.

"Max! I came home early to surprise you!"

"Amanda—you're home!" I said, delighted when she pressed her body against mine. "I thought you were coming tomorrow." I closed my eyes and buried my face in her hair, which had a delicious fragrance of lilac.

She planted kisses on my face, squealing like a child at a birthday party. "Max! Great news! I'm going to be in a movie!"

"Wonderful! Tell me about it." She pulled me inside our apartment and I dropped my bags.

"Max, oh, Max, I'm so happy!" she giggled, swirling us around our living room, our arms locked around each other. I bumped into the coffee table, fell back, and landed on our sofa, pulling Amanda on top of me. We laughed, fumbling to sit up.

She straddled me and smothered me with more kisses. It felt great.

"Tell me, tell me! When did you find out?"

"My agent called this morning, just before left for the airport. I was going to call you, but I wanted to tell you face to face," she giggled, her energy unleashed. She squirmed her body against me. "I've called everyone—my mom, my aunt and uncle, your parents, my drama teacher, my sorority sisters. I'm so excited—I could almost wet my pants!"

I laughed and struggled to sit up. "Hey, better not. This is a new sofa."

"Okay, okay. I'll settle down," she said, moving off me so we could sit side by side on the sofa.

"Tell me everything. What's the movie?"

She took a deep breath and exhaled, calming down to tell me her news. She pressed her hands on my cheeks and leaned close so our eyes were just a few inches away. "Remember I told you I read for three movies in development?"

"Sure. One was a historical drama about England, another a thriller, and a comedy, I think. Which one is it?"

"The one I wanted: the romantic comedy. It's been green-lit and starts shooting in a month in Vancouver. The director had me read for the female lead!"

"The lead in your first role! That's incredible!"

She fanned her hand in front of her blushing face. "Whoo, let me catch my breath. The title's just so-so: *Every Day Is Sunday*. I'm cast with Liam McGregor, that hot new Scottish actor. He called just before you got home to congratulate me."

"Honey, that's great. This could be your big break."

"Do you mind if I'm in Vancouver for a couple of months?" she asked, pleading like a child asking for a cookie.

"Of course not. I'll come out when the season's over."

"I want you to come! I'll be so nervous. You'll like the direc- tor. He's a Red Sox fan and remembers when you got drafted. He can't wait to meet you. I promised him you'd give him an autograph."

"That's a deal—anything to help you."

* * *

I went to Vancouver in September after the regular baseball season ended. I'd had my best year, playing regularly, but was disappointed that the Red Sox finished fourth in the American League Eastern Division.

The opening scenes of *Every Day Is Sunday* were shot at an indoor set in Vancouver. It was my first time on a movie set. The energy and chaos were amusing: people scrambling around like mice in a cage; the director barking instructions to actors and to crews moving dollies with bright lights and cameras around the set; everyone jabbering on headsets; staff touching up actors' and actresses' makeup and adjusting their clothes and hair before the director yelled out, "Action . . . filming!"

It was controlled anarchy, but everyone knew what they were supposed to be doing.

I was proud to observe Amanda at work, knowing her lines and blocking, asking for guidance from crews, behaving like an experienced actress. Her acting looked natural—no nerves, fear, or uncertainty. She was a pro already.

During a break the first day, the director came over to introduce himself, wearing a Red Sox cap. We fist-bumped, and he gave me a big smile and said, "Hey, Max! A thrill to meet you. Had a great season, and an All-Star already. I'm impressed."

We spent a couple of minutes talking "inside baseball" and analyzing the teams in the playoffs. He was from Maine and had gone to Fenway when he was a UMass student. I pulled an autographed baseball out of my coat pocket and handed it to him; he beamed like a Little Leaguer. We became instant friends.

They finished the movie in three months, shooting downtown

scenes in Vancouver and outdoor scenes at Whistler ski resort with the first snow of the season on the slopes. We went out to dinner every night, joining the crew and actors, who were enthused about their good fortune to be working in the movie industry, with all the creativity, travel, and talented people.

I was a bit envious, but I felt the same joy playing professional baseball and having talented ballplayers as friends. Amanda and I were both lucky to be working in exciting professions that gave us joy and meaning every day.

Every Day Is Sunday was entered at the Sundance festival the next spring. Word of Amanda's performance got around, and she got calls from directors who asked what roles she was looking for next.

* * *

My parents flew to Boston to spend Christmas with us. Amanda made a trip to see her mother in January, and then we started looking around for a home to buy. December and January flew by too fast, and by February we were moving in two directions to pursue our demanding careers.

I went to spring training in February. My dad came and spent ten days. Amanda was in New York for meetings with directors, acting lessons, and auditions for roles on Broadway.

It was the first spring training I didn't have injuries, and I felt like I'd have another good season. I was in the starting lineup when we opened the season in April at Yankee Stadium. It was a cold, windy, rainy three-day series, two day games and one night game. I got a hit in each game but was glad to get into the locker room at the end of the games and take a hot shower. Baseball season is too long; it should start in mid-April rather than early April, when players and fans have to put up with frigid temperatures, rain, snow, and even blizzards.

My parents and Amanda were in the stands. We went to dinner every night in New York. Mom and Dad were overjoyed, telling us we were lucky to have a good marriage and exciting careers at such young ages.

In May, Amanda left for London for her next movie, a thriller with a leading British actor. She was gone most of the summer, shooting in Scotland and Wales, and on a trawler in the North Sea. She called me often, telling me how much she liked British actors and going to pubs with them after daily shoots. She was having the time of her life, traveling to interesting places and meeting young British actors and actresses.

She spent two weeks filming in London but was disappointed that she didn't have time to see the sights. After they wrapped in London, she went with actor friends to see a matinee performance of *The Full Monty* at the Noel Coward Theatre in the West End. After the play, they had dinner near Trafalgar Square and ended the night at a Hyde Park pub. She called the next day to tell me it was one of the most memorable days of her life.

Amanda didn't make it to many games that season. I spent the summer on team charter flights to the West Coast and swings through the Midwest and the East Coast—no places as glamorous as those in which Amanda was spending her time. She was seeing the world; I was living in hotels and on planes and playing in noisy ballparks every day. I missed Amanda every night I crawled into bed alone—in Boston, Tampa, Chicago, New York, Detroit, Anaheim, and Oakland. I wanted us to be together, not living thousands of miles apart. We had exciting careers, but they were keeping us from enjoying our marriage.

8
____

Amanda spent most of the winter in New York and Miami for her next movie, another romantic comedy about a handsome young Cuban guitar player who became a love interest to three women who competed to help him launch his career as a musician. I read the script and thought the story was a bit lame. But what did I know?

Amanda's character won out in the end. She and the Cuban became lovers, and the credits ran as they were walking down a South Beach boardwalk at sunset, hand in hand, the Cuban with his guitar over his back. Not my kind of movie, but such films were popular among younger viewers who were buying tickets and paying Amanda's salary.

I went to spring training in February, healthy but distracted, worried about how much time Amanda and I were spending apart. She was excited about her new movie and the good press she was getting as a rising star. I was also anxious about beginning the long baseball season, hoping injuries wouldn't bench me.

The first week of spring training was about reuniting with my Boston teammates, as well as meeting the latest crop of college draftees eager to impress coaches. I was taking batting practice one morning when our infield coach, Ryan Webber, stood outside the cage watching me blast line drives, dropping them in the gap between outfielders. Line drives into the gap can turn into doubles or triples if the ball runs to the outfield wall. Coach Webber stood behind me, giving me "attaboys" as I finished my turn in the cage after stroking three line drives down the foul line —drives that could mean extra bases.

"You're hot, Max. I like how you're placing your hits. Keep that up and you'll have another great season."

Ryan "The Rocket" Webber had been one of my idols when he played for Cincinnati. He was a stocky third baseman who could snag a grounder and fire across the diamond, his arm a bazooka. Ryan had won five Golden Gloves and had a lifetime .304 batting average. He played in three All-Star games and was Most Valuable Player in one, scoring the winning run with a homer.

I'd watched Rocket play on TV when I was in junior high school and had wanted to be just like him one day. I marveled at how easy he made everything look. Sign of a real pro.

Rocket's career ended badly in the eighth inning of a meaningless September night game when the Reds were ahead of the last-place Pirates 9-2. He dove for a foul ball behind third base with his glove out. Just as he snagged the ball, his chin slammed into the dugout railing. He shattered his jaw, and it was wired for six months.

When Rocket showed up for spring training the following season, the trainer fitted him with a special batting helmet that made him look like a football halfback. But Rocket was jinxed by fear of reinjuring his jaw; he cringed every time a pitcher fired an inside fastball. His confidence gone, he retired at age thirty-seven and became a minor league manager with the Red Sox.

As I came out of the batting cage, Rocket slapped me on the

back. "You look better every season, Max. You've been working out over the winter, haven't you?"

"Sure have, Rocket. Running sprints, lifting weights, and playing pickup basketball," I said as he followed me down the first base line to get my glove for infield practice. "Boston's gyms are loaded with former college players in all sports. They mop up the floor with me, but I put up a jump shot once in a while."

"Yeah," he said, "but you can hit a ninety-five-mile-per-hour fastball, and they can't."

Rocket was one of the coaches everyone listened to, not just because of his stellar career, but also because of his common sense and wisdom. His body looked like it was carved from a redwood, with long, sinewy arms that could still toss a ball from second base over the fence. A buttery roll of fat over his belt made Rocket look like Buddha in a baseball uniform.

We looked out at the field, where teammates and rookies were stretching and running wind sprints, getting ready for our first intrasquad game. Every spring, new talent showed up with stars in their eyes, hoping to impress coaches and get called up from the minors during the season.

The new talent, recent draftees and minor league veterans, pumped me for fielding tips and asked what it was like to play in the majors. I shared a few tips, mostly things they should have known. But they were after my job, so I kept a few things to myself.

Rocket put an arm around my shoulder as we walked toward first base, where I'd left my glove. "So, Max, you haven't had trouble with injuries the last couple seasons. What's your secret?"

"Just hard work, keeping off weight, and working with a personal trainer at my gym. He's been great. Got me to take supplements and watch my diet—lots of protein—and keep away from salt, sugar, and fats. My goal is to make it through the year without injuries. I hate sitting on the bench."

"Yeah, it's a bitch riding the pines," Rocket said, reaching into a back pocket for a pack of chewing tobacco. He pinched a plug and stuck it in his cheek. "You know, Max, I like you," he said in his slow, South Carolina drawl. "You remind me of myself when I was your age. You hustle every play. You're hungry and you've got the tools. You could play a few more seasons if you stay healthy."

"Thanks, coach. That's a real honor coming from you." I told him about watching him play when he was an All-Star.

He chewed on the plug, squinting in the morning sunlight and tipping back his hat. "You've been playing how long, Max, four, five seasons?"

"This is my sixth."

"How many years you think you got left?" he asked, drawling the word left like it was stuck on his tongue.

"Long as I can, coach. I'd love to play another six or eight years."

Rocket didn't answer right away as he watched rookies fielding grounders. He winced every time one of them let a ball get by or overthrew to first base. I thought he was distracted, but then he said, "What if you don't make it that long, Max? Lots of guys start going soft when they hit thirty or thirty-one. Hope that doesn't happen to you."

I grimaced. "Yeah, I think about that, coach," I confessed, scuffing the dirt with my toe. I could tell something was on his mind. We'd exchanged mostly small talk in the past. I appreciated his taking an interest in my career. He was a minor league manager, so spring training was the only time we saw much of each other.

"I don't have to tell you that busloads of talented guys show up every spring. College ball isn't what it was when I was getting in the game. Colleges are farm teams for us; they turn out fantastic players every season. They're faster, stronger, and hungry. Reeeaaaalll hungry," he said, dragging out the word. "Even at my best, I don't think I could have made it against these new college guys. Competition's the most intense I've ever seen."

"Don't have to tell me about it, coach. I see them too. A couple of these rookies could make the lineup this summer. It's a young man's game. I'm twenty-eight and not getting any younger."

"Yup," he said, rolling the plug of tobacco from one cheek to the other and then spitting a glob onto the grass.

"Let me tell you something, Junior. Hope you don't mind me calling you Junior. I only call guys that who remind me of when my dad called me Junior."

"No, that's fine. Call me what you like, coach. I can learn from you."

"Okay. Hope you don't mind me telling you a few facts about having a successful career in baseball and life."

"No, please. I want to know."

"Here it is: the damn bitter truth. One day, oh, a few years down the road, you'll be out of the game. You'll pick up the sports page, and your name won't be there. Saddest day of your life. You're not playing ball anymore. You'll think everyone forgot about you. No one will give a damn about you, except maybe at autograph shows, where you'll earn three hundred dollars to sign balls and tell tall tales to ten-year-old boys and their dads."

Rocket spit another glob into the grass and spread it around with his cleats. "Finish college yet?" he asked.

"Almost. I'll get my degree next winter. Just have two business classes left. I skipped a couple years when I was first married and started playing ball."

He looked at me like a principal scolding a student. "What do you do with your healthy paycheck?"

I shrugged, feeling a little uneasy. Even though I'd studied business, I hadn't paid much attention to my own finances. "A little of this, a little of that. I bought myself a Porsche when I got my signing bonus. My wife and I have new Audis. I bought my parents a new SUV after I signed. I gave my mother-in-law fifty thousand dollars to fix up her house. My wife and I took winter vacations to the Bahamas and Mexico. I travel during the winter to see my wife when she's on location. We took a European vacation after she finished a movie over there."

"Yeah, she's the actress. Pretty lady. You're lucky. I saw her on the speedboat in that English movie with the airplane chase. She's probably knocking down good money."

"She is. Probably catch up to me one of these years."

"How much you saving from all that loot?"

"Not much, I guess." I had half a million dollars in a couple of CDs waiting until I found something to buy. I'd had my eye on a sailboat in Fort Lauderdale, but the price was a little steep, $300,000. I had the papers at home but hadn't signed yet.

Rocket scowled, spit another gob in the dirt, and wiped his chin. "Get serious about your money before it's too late. Don't be like me. I pissed away four million dollars on three wives, two divorces, fast cars, girlfriends, gambling, and booze. I had a great time, you betcha, but I dug myself a financial hole deeper than the Grand Canyon. I'm broke as a one-legged banjo player. I didn't get my college degree even though I promised my parents I would. But my life was crazy fun when I was in my twenties, livin' high on the hog, running in the fast lane where all the action was. Stupid, I know, but I was young and foolish and thought the easy money would never stop flowing. Then I got married, had a couple kids, got divorced, gave the wife and kids half my salary, got married again, another kid, another divorce, half the rest of my salary went to them. I lost a bundle in bad restaurant deals, real estate schemes, oil and gas ventures —all sorts of scams that 'friends' were throwing at me. They weren't really friends, just phonies who saw me as a soft touch."

"I know what you mean, coach. I had a couple restaurant offers come my way but didn't go in. I'm glad; they went belly-up."

"Don't be a sucker, Max. I wish someone had told me about watching my money when I was your age. I wouldn't be in the mess I am now. If I can't hang on to my shitty job as a minor league manager, I'll end up selling cars. I had a couple tryouts as a sportscaster, but they passed on me. My English isn't what you learned in school; I sounded like a Carolina hayseed with a piece of straw in his mouth when I auditioned."

I chuckled. I'd heard Rocket's accent a few times when he was chewing out younger players for messing up. He was funny, using colorful profanity and mangled metaphors, like you'd hear on the old *Hee Haw* TV show. Everyone loved his goofy, home-spun sense of humor.

"You'd be a great announcer, Rocket. You know the game and how to tell stories. I've heard you in the locker room. You're a funny guy."

"Naw, don't give me that, Max," he said, spitting another glob in the dirt. "Those stories I tell in the locker room can't be repeated in public. Growing up hardscrabble in Oklahoma, I learned early how to tell stories and get folks to laugh—with me, sometimes at me. It came natural, but it's not a talent that can get you a fat paycheck on those TV sports shows. During auditions for radio and TV, they loved my baseball stories, but I came across like I was in the locker room, using too much baseball lingo. And I wasn't quick on my feet when they fired questions at me. I hired a PR guy to work with me, but the stations all said, 'Thanks, but no thanks. See you around.'"

"Sorry, coach. I still think you would have been good in the booth."

"Too late for that now. They were the only jobs that paid

decent; all the other choices were pathetic: selling insurance, greeter at casinos and resorts, hitting the rubber-chicken circuit for Kiwanis and Rotary."

He leaned over and spit another gob of black juice on the ground.

Rocket was quiet for a minute and then put his hand on my shoulder. "I like you, Max. You're a good ballplayer and have a real future ahead of you. You have the brains to be successful after you hang up your spikes."

"Thanks, I appreciate that."

"Don't make the mistakes I did. Get your schooling. Buy real estate. Find a smart guy to sort out your finances. Save money, as much as you can. Think of your future, not just what you're batting average will be this year."

"My wife and I have talked about buying a house, but we've been busy with our careers."

"Do it. Soon. Look ahead a few years. You'll need a real job one day. Start planning or you'll end up like me and every sorry honcho out here who thinks the easy money will last forever. Half the coaches out here wish they'd been smart with their easy money. We look at you guys with the million-dollar contracts and know you'll probably end up like us. Money comes too easy when you're young and healthy. Take my word for it: Neither will last. You'll get slow, old, and fat one day, just like me. Don't be stupid, too."

9

———————

The conversation with Rocket motivated me to get serious about our finances. When Amanda returned to Boston in April, we met with a financial advisor who advised us to buy a home, get life insurance, and start retirement plans.

Amanda called a friend from her TV station job who lived in Wellesley, Massachusetts. She recommended we check out homes there. She referred us to her real estate agent, and after a couple of phone calls, we drove to Wellesley. We toured four homes one morning before a night game, the last a three-story, four-bedroom, stone and wood colonial that backed onto a wooded park. We loved the colonial exterior, with its pillared portico, covered porch, and dormer windows. But the spacious interior was what sold us: two rooms that could be turned into offices; a large, modern kitchen; a cathedral ceiling and polished wooden floors in the living room; and a huge master bedroom on the second floor. The backyard patio was perfect for summer parties, with a stone fence and Italian flagstone.

We signed a contract for the house with a $300,000 down

payment that I had been planning to put down on a sailboat. This was a smarter way to put our money to work for us. I called Rocket to tell him the good news.

"Smart boy, Max," he said. "Sounds like a nice little nest for you and your lovely wife. You owe me dinner next time I'm in Boston."

"Deal, Rocket. I'll give you a house tour and you can stay in our guest room. Bring your wife, spend a couple nights, and check out Wellesley."

"Naw, just send me a picture, Max," he drawled. "Wellesley's one of those places where latte-sipping liberals sit around and talk about keeping us hillbillies from moving in. I'd freak out your neighbors if they saw me hanging around. Bring down their housing values."

In May, during our next home stand, Amanda and I closed on the Wellesley house. After we signed stacks of paperwork and legal documents, our real estate agent presented us with keys and a gift basket of wine, champagne, cheeses, gourmet olives, and fruit.

We drove to our new home with the backseat crammed with new pillows, sheets, and towels to add homey touches, and then we waited for a furniture truck to deliver our new bed. I had a night game but wanted to enjoy our new home before leaving for Fenway.

I unlocked the front door for the first time, picked up Amanda, and carried her across the threshold. She burst out laughing and smothered me in kisses. "Max, you're so old fashioned—I love it! Our own home!"

We threw pillows on the polished floor of our living room, poured champagne, and sampled goodies from the gift basket until the truck showed up with our new king-size bed.

For the occasion, Amanda wore a new yellow and blue dress that clung to her trim body. Her Los Angeles hairdresser had cut her hair fashionably short with a part on one side. A makeup artist had styled her eyebrows and lashes so they accented her pale green eyes. She looked like a model posing for a photographer to shoot a fashion magazine cover.

"Max, I love our home!" Amanda giggled as we sat cross-legged on pillows. "We're going to be so happy here!"

"Who knows, in a year or so, if we redecorate the bedroom next to ours, we might have a baby join us. Wouldn't that be great!"

Amanda squeezed my hand, trying to calm me down. "One day it'll happen, but let's get used to our home by ourselves first. There'll be time to talk about starting a family later. You'll be a great dad. I know you will."

After the furniture truck drove away, Amanda gave me that look, turning her head slowly, her gaze moving up the curved stairway to our second-floor master bedroom.

"Hey, honey," she winked at me and purred in a low, sexy voice. "How about a little 'whoopee', in our new bed in our new home? Whaddaya think?"

I made a face like a clown who was surprised when a rabbit jumped out of his hat. "Wow!" I exclaimed, glancing at my watch. "Just time enough before I have to leave for Fenway. Race you!"

We jumped up from the pillows, slipping on the polished floor in our stocking feet and bumping into each other as we dashed up the steps. When we reached the bedroom, we threw sheets and pillows onto the bed, tore off our clothes, and jumped into the bed without tucking in the sheets.

Our lovemaking was brief but wild as we got tangled in the loose sheets, rolling over each other, almost falling off, laughing at our uninhibited passion.

"Ooh, that was sooo delicious, and fun," she cooed when it was over too quickly. "You're the best lover," she said, our clenched, naked bodies damp with sex and lust. "As good as our first lovemaking at NDSU. We ripped up the sheets then too, remember?"

"Whoo, do I ever," I gasped. "Nothing like the first time. Can we do this again tonight?"

She pushed me off, our damp bodies making a suction pop as I rolled away. "Hey," she said, reaching up to kiss me. "You gotta get to your game, big boy. Don't have to hit a home run tonight. You've already hit a grand slam!"

We laughed like kids on a playground as I fumbled out of bed and ran into the bathroom. "I won't need batting practice either," I said as I turned on the shower. "Gotta save my strength for the game."

She followed me into the shower, grabbing the soap and lathering my body, arousing me again. She purred in that low, sexy voice that I loved. "Hey, Max," she said slowly, "everyone in the locker room will know what you've been doing this afternoon. Your grin has 'just gotten laid' written all over it."

While I was at our night game, Amanda unpacked boxes in the living room and arranged our master suite for the first night in our new home. She prepared a candlelight dinner of shrimp and filets, which we ate on our new dining table while looking out at the neighborhood through our undraped floor-to-ceiling windows.

The dishes remained in the sink after dinner; we ran up the stairs and made love again in our new bed, this time with sheets tucked and blankets to pull over us. We giggled and shared pillow talk until two in the morning, when we fell asleep, exhausted but overjoyed at being new homeowners.

It was one of the happiest days of our marriage.

* * *

Our futures seemed boundless. But the mood of unbounded optimism was fleeting. Over the next year, the things I held most dear started to unravel.

In June, I got hit on the elbow by an inside fastball and missed ten games. In July, a base runner tore my left calf muscle when he slid into second with spikes raised as I took a throw to start a double play.

Our team physician stitched up my calf, and I hobbled around on crutches for two weeks, moody and depressed. I returned to the lineup after rehabilitation and played hurt. In my third game back, I dove to snag a line drive and felt a hot knife stab deep into my calf. The trainer ran onto the field, where I lay in the dirt, gripping my calf, which was torn open again. Blood seeped through my uniform. I almost cried from the excruciating pain.

It was September before I returned to the lineup. I didn't steal another base after my injury. The previous two seasons, I had led our team in steals and was third in runs scored. My injuries this season cost me seventy games. My batting average dropped to .242. I scored only thirty-five runs with no doubles or triples after the calf injury.

I was on the injured reserve roster for a month and watched two young infielders take turns at second base. They'd had stellar college careers and a couple of good seasons in the minors, like I had. They were after my job. If I didn't get healthy, one of them would take it.

If I was lucky, I had a couple more years to play. Remembering the talk with Rocket, I dreaded the day in the future when my name wouldn't show up in the sports pages.

That winter, I took a business course at Babson College in Wellesley to finish my undergraduate degree. I enjoyed the intellectual stimulation of reading textbooks and debating with the professor and fellow students. It was one of the few things I enjoyed during that cold, snowy Boston winter.

Amanda wasn't in Boston much after we moved into our Wellesley home. She was in Los Angeles shooting a new movie with a well-known director. Because of his fame, the movie was mentioned frequently in the trades, and Amanda was featured in photo spreads as a young star on the rise.

I had mixed emotions about the media attention Amanda was getting. I was proud she was doing well, but I felt envious of her glamorous social life. While she was going to parties, premieres, and dinners, I was staying up late reading biographies and sleeping alone in the king-size bed in our new home.

I worried about Amanda. She was beautiful, fun to be with, and liked to flirt. Her sex appeal was a magnet for men. She played to her strength.

How do you keep a marriage going when you don't see your spouse for weeks at a time? I felt our marriage was adrift, like a raft in the ocean.

We'd spend occasional weekends together in Boston or LA. Our reunions had once been wildly uninhibited: tearing off our clothes, jumping into bed, and making passionate love like randy teenagers. But after we bought our home and settled into a more conventional domestic life, we began to behave more like friends than lovers.

When Amanda was in Wellesley, she'd spend her days in our study, reading scripts and talking on the phone to West Coast agents, producers, and actors. There was no end of calls with media requests for interviews and party invitations in New York and LA.

We rarely ate dinner at home. Instead, we'd go out with friends or teammates, talking more to them than to each other. Drives back home were subdued, same as in bed. We made love, but it was a formality, like a polite handshake, a ritual before rolling over and falling asleep. Pillow talk was a thing of the past.

Our marriage was getting stale. I hated to admit it. But we didn't talk about the chill that had settled in.

I worried about how Amanda was spending time in LA. We exchanged phone calls and e-mails every day but usually talked about mundane details regarding work. I could sense a distance, as if neither one of us knew what to say. Conversations were polite and almost formal. Something was missing. The spark that had ignited our marriage in the first years was gone. For the first time in my life, I had days of sadness and depression. I spent more time alone than I should have. I knew friends would recognize my mood change and start asking questions that I was too embarrassed to answer honestly.

My fear was that Amanda was having an affair. But I wasn't going to reveal my suspicion. I wasn't her meal ticket anymore. She was making good money but not sharing how she was investing or saving.

When we did our taxes before I left for spring training, I was surprised at how much Amanda was earning. Not as much as I was making, but close.

"I'm thinking of buying a place in LA," she said out of the blue when we left our CPA's office after signing our 1040 form. We had a brief conversation in the car that confirmed that the rift in our marriage was obvious.

"Oh," I said. "What did you have in mind?"

"I like working in LA. After you retire from baseball, we could live there."

"Mmm. Not sure I want to live in LA. I love our Wellesley home and being close to Boston. Jump on the T, and we're downtown in a half hour."

She shook her head. "Brrr. Winters are cold in New England. I like the LA weather. Plus there are tons of things to do in Southern California. We could take vacations in Hawaii every winter. My friends have condos and timeshares on Maui and the Big Island. We could go anytime."

"But I'd miss the seasons if we lived in LA," I protested, unsettled about this new information about her not wanting to stay in Wellesley. "There's so much history in New England. Plus, there's all these places to visit in Maine, New Hampshire, and Vermont."

She had an impatient look on her face, as if she didn't care what I thought. "Well, I know you like New England, but it's cold except for a couple months in summer."

Stalemate.

I started the car and drove out of the parking lot. Neither one of us spoke. We didn't want an argument, and we both knew a major issue had surfaced that didn't allow for compromise. If an argument started, it might veer into the state of our marriage, which was becoming a minefield of unspoken emotions.

When we walked into our house, Amanda headed straight for the kitchen and turned to look at me in the living room. There was a divider between the kitchen and living room—not the only partition separating us.

"Max, buying a place in LA makes sense," she said, a firmness in her voice. "No use keeping all that cash in my savings account. Real estate is a great investment in LA, especially in good neighborhoods."

Her mind was made up. Owning a home on each coast meant we'd have a country between us. I sensed that an argument about her decision was futile. "I'm sure it is," I said as we stared across the divider at each other with no emotion showing on either of our faces. We had both been happy when we had bought our Wellesley home, but her choice to buy another home across the country had none of the joy we'd known before.

"A real estate agent showed me a cute bungalow in West Hollywood," she said, breaking away and opening the refrigerator door. She looked inside, not at me. "I'd like to make a down payment on it next week. What do you think?"

I was stunned. She hadn't told me about the real estate agent even though she'd been home a month. "Our advisor says real estate is usually a good investment," I said. "I suppose it's a good idea."

"Good," she said. She turned to look at me across the divider, a glimmer of satisfaction on her face. "Next time you come out, I'll show you the place. You'd like it. It's in a charming neighborhood—lots of shops, ethnic restaurants, markets, and an old movie theater. A few friends live nearby, so it's not like I'd be by myself."

10

———

In July, the Red Sox made a swing to the West Coast to play the teams in the American League West: the Seattle Mariners, the Oakland A's, and the California Angels. We flew from Oakland the morning after a night game and had a few hours before playing the Angels in another night game, just enough time to see Amanda's new West Hollywood home.

A couple of younger teammates were in the hotel lobby with me while I waited for Amanda to pick me up. They were new to the Red Sox and hadn't met Amanda. They were as eager as puppies to meet a real Hollywood actress.

On schedule, Amanda pulled into the hotel's circular drive-way, tipped a valet, and made an entrance into the lobby as if she were on camera. She looked smashing: very tanned, sunglasses on top of her head, and wearing a short, swishy skirt, a pastel blue silk blouse, and open-toed high heels that accented her long, tanned legs, which were the color of cocoa.

"Hey, good-looking," she said, reaching up to kiss me and give me a hug. "Are these your new teammates?"

"Yeah, they bribed me with a hundred dollars to meet you," I said, winking at them. "Amanda, this is Chet from Birmingham and Ollie—Oliver—from Florida."

"Hi, fellas!" she said, flashing a warm smile and reaching out to shake their hands. "You ballplayers are all soooo handsome—and young. How old are you?"

"I'm twenty-four," Chet said.

"I'm twenty-three," Ollie said nervously.

She looped her arm through mine. "You probably won't believe this, guys, but when Max was your age, I had to fight off girls with a bat! Seriously! He's still the handsomest guy on the team, but now he's an old married guy and talks about the stock market, real estate, and business, like men in their fifties. Take my advice: Stay young and have fun as long as you can. And don't hang around old guys who talk about the stock market and real estate."

Chet and Ollie chuckled and looked more at ease. Amanda had broken the ice with a gentle touch of humor. She knew how to charm men, disarming them with her good looks and lack of guile.

"You guys going to win tonight?" she asked. "Don't lose another one in the ninth, like you did in Oakland last night. That was a heartbreaker."

"We'll win tonight. You can count on it," Chet said. "Hey, ah, Amanda, ah, could I . . . you know . . . have an autograph? I've never met a real actress before." Neither man took their eyes off of Amanda, not gawking but clearly enamored.

"You bet," she said. She reached into her purse and pulled out two pocket-sized color photos. She took out a pen, auto-graphed both pictures, and handed them to her new admirers.

"This is so cool!" Ollie said, his eyes widening. "That's a great picture, Amanda."

"Thanks. It was nice to meet you both." As if following a script, Amanda turned to me. "Max, we'd better run. I don't want you to miss tonight's game."

She turned to Chet and Ollie. "I'll be at the game tonight with a couple girlfriends. If you want, we could all go out for a drink after the game. Okay, Max?"

"Sure, of course," I said.

"Really?! That would be great! Are they actresses too?" Chet said, babbling like a fourteen-year-old boy who'd just met a homecoming queen.

"One of them is. The other is a designer. They're both fun and pretty," she said with a wink.

"Oh, boy, wait until my brother hears about this!" Chet said, barely containing his glee. "He couldn't believe it when I told him I was going to meet you. He just saw your new movie, Bahama Sunrise. I'm going as soon as we're back in Boston."

"Good. I hope you like it. See you tonight, guys!" she said, giving them a quick wave and taking my hand.

"Hey, don't get stuck in traffic, Max," Chet called out as we reached the revolving door. "We need you in the lineup tonight."

They waved, smiles across their faces like they'd won the lottery. "Take care of Max, Amanda!" Ollie shouted.

When I reached Amanda's new black Audi with tinted windows and a sunroof, I looked back and saw Ollie and Chet ogling Amanda's photo, nudging each other and giggling like little boys.

Amanda drove out of the driveway, waved at the valet, and flicked a blinker to get onto the freeway ramp.

"Nice fellas," she said as she accelerated, her Audi racing up the ramp and slipping into a space between cars. She drove with the ease of a housewife ironing a shirt—effortless, relaxed, routine.

"I hope they're not married. I didn't see any wedding rings."

"Nope, both single."

"Good. Don't want to get in trouble with any wives."

Amanda reached over and squeezed my thigh. "Max, I'm so thrilled to have you see my home! I've only been in it three days.

The last month has been crazy-crazy-crazy with painters, decorators, and landscapers working nonstop to get ready for your visit. I hope you like it. It's such a cool house." She was bubbling with excitement, the happiest I'd seen her in a long time.

The day was sunny and warm, and Amanda navigated the freeway traffic effortlessly, like a true Angeleno, changing lanes to take advantage of openings, unfazed by being in heavy traffic with trucks, SUVs, and sports cars traveling at high speeds with only a few feet between bumpers.

As she drove, I tried to relax, gazing out at the vast Los Angeles urban sprawl of freeways, high-rises, office buildings, residential developments, shopping centers, car dealerships, and construction in all directions. LA is too congested for me, but Amanda seemed as comfortable as if she were in a garden watering flowers. I was amazed at her poise. After half an hour, I could see a sliver of the blue Pacific Ocean and airplanes taking off and landing at LAX.

Amanda exited I-5 onto Santa Monica Boulevard and drove down Sunset Strip, briefing me on the background of the clubs, restaurants, and shops that lined the strip. She turned off at Harper Avenue and drove past hotels, condos, apartments, and office complexes until we reached a quiet street lined with tall palm trees and blooming jacaranda.

"We're getting close," she said. You like the neighborhood?"

"Sure," I said, trying to sound enthused. But there was little open space; buildings were crowded next to each other. I saw limited green space. Parking lots were full of shiny new cars, and every parking space on the streets was filled.

She braked in the middle of a residential street and pulled into a driveway in front of a one-car garage.

"Here we are, Max—our little West Hollywood bungalow. What do you think?"

It was cute but tiny: one story with white shutters on the windows, freshly painted yellow stucco, and a postage-stamp-sized lawn with camellias, begonias, banana palm, and colorful lantana. Two-car garages were larger than her pretty little box.

She took my hand and led me up a stone path to the front door. When she unlocked it, she bowed slightly, motioning for me to enter, like an artist showing her latest creation. We entered a foyer that led into her living room, which was smaller than our study in Wellesley.

Amanda waited for me to look around. It took a moment for my eyes to adjust from the bright sunlight to the subdued interior light. She walked around, running her fingers over the furniture. "I love the design of the new Eames chairs and ottomans. The sofa is a Krefeld. Very modern looking, don't you think?"

"Yes, they are."

"The glass coffee table looks good by the fireplace. I had someone clean it out and paint it to match the furniture. I haven't used it yet, of course, but it will be cozy in the winter, don't you think?"

"Yes, very attractive, stylish."

"And how about the bamboo ceiling fan?" she pointed to a fan that was only a foot above my head. Our cathedral ceilings in Wellesley were probably fifteen feet higher.

"My decorator helped me pick out the thin metal lamps. They look like modern sculpture, don't you think? They were a little expensive, but they add vertical texture to the room," she said with a laugh. "At least, that's what my decorator said. She's really creative. Like she said, with a small living room, you want some verticality."

"Yes," I agreed.

We walked across gray carpet, leaving faint footprints on our way to an alcove that led to the kitchen. The alcove was tiny, with a tea trolley and an antique Chinese porcelain vase in the corner. A glass door off the alcove opened onto a patio with a wooden fence separating her from neighbors.

"The kitchen was just finished, so I haven't fixed any meals yet," she said, running her hand over the green marble-topped counter. "I have a Sub-Zero range, a double-wide refrigerator and freezer, and a center counter with a small sink for chopping and dicing vegetables. There wasn't a lot of room to work with, so my designer put in a wooden rack above the counter to hang pots and pans."

A vase of fresh-cut flowers was next to a glassed wine cabinet by the sink. Amanda opened the accompanying envelope and read it.

"Oh, isn't that nice. She sent me flowers and gave me a wine cabinet as a housewarming gift." Amanda opened the wine cabinet. "And look, Max, she gave us wine, too! Isn't she sweet?"

"A nice touch."

Amanda took out one bottle, then another, reading the labels.

"French bordeaux and Italian chianti. What nice gifts. Shall I open a bottle?"

"Sure, why not."

She dug in a drawer for a wine opener and popped the cork of the Bordeaux. I found two wineglasses in a cabinet. "Not too much, honey," I said. "I've got a game tonight."

She poured a few ounces for each of us, and we raised our glasses in a toast.

"To our new home, Max. Isn't it just perfect?"

We sipped, kissed across our glasses, and finished our small pours. "Now, let me show you the bedroom!" Amanda said.

She led me down a carpeted hallway to the two bedrooms and bathroom. On one wall were two Leroy Neiman prints: one of boxers in the ring, the other of a baseball game. Across from them was an abstract painting in broad brushstrokes of yellow, green, red, and blue that looked like they'd been flung onto the canvas by an angry chimpanzee.

Amanda's bedroom would have fit in a corner of our Wellesley master bedroom. The only furniture was a dresser and a platform bed with a canopy. The bed was covered with designer pillows in lavender silk.

"My decorator recommended Laura Ashley wallpaper, which I love. And the sheets are eight-hundred-thread Egyptian cotton —the most luxurious you can find."

I smiled as naturally as I could, turned, and took one step into the bathroom: Italian tile with a glassed-in shower and a small Jacuzzi. The counter had two washbasins, and above them was a mirror that went to the ceiling. Two people could squeeze together between the sink and the wall, but one would have to move out if the other opened the shower door. I felt like I was in a sleeping car on a train.

When I returned to the bedroom, Amanda was in front of her walk-in closet. "The bedroom's a little small, but I wanted a big closet for my clothes and shoes and other stuff."

One-half of the closet was lined with metal hangers holding stylish blouses, short sundresses, and slacks. Next to these were formal, floor-length dresses, appropriate for Hollywood premieres when starlets emerge from black limousines to parade down red carpets before flashing cameras, TV lights, and screaming fans.

The other half had stacked shelves crammed with high heels, dressy flats, stilettos, loafers, slippers, sandals, and boots. On the top shelf was a row of hats in eclectic styles and colors: beaded types, like from the flapper era; wide-brimmed formal hats like women wear at the Kentucky Derby; and numerous sun hats, some with colored ribbons. I was amazed; I'd seen Amanda wear hats only at weddings and special parties.

"I started collecting hats when I came to LA," she said when she saw me staring at her hat collection. "What do you think? Kind of and cute, aren't they? I don't wear them often, just for special occasions. I get them from costume designers who'll make three or four of a style, but the director only wants one, and the designer sells the rest. I get a special deal—at least, that's what the designers say."

She took me over to a glass patio door, parted the curtain, and opened the door. We stepped out into the sunlight. "I really wanted a pool, but in this neighborhood they cost a fortune. Maybe next time I can get a pool. My landscaper tore out the lawn, kept the orange trees, and put in a gazebo and koi pond. I love the sound of the water over the stones."

I gazed at the fountain with water falling over smooth stones into the koi pond. Between the orange trees was a latticed gazebo covered in blue morning glory vines. She was right; there was no room for a pool larger than a long bathtub.

"I like your patio. Nice and shady with the orange trees," I said. "And quiet. The waterfall is soothing. Do you think you will spend much time out here?"

"I hope to—when I'm home."

Amanda had done a nice job decorating her place in her own style, but I didn't feel at home there. Our traditional Wellesley home was more my style, a mansion compared to her bungalow, with more rooms; long, wide hallways; natural lighting; skylights; and floor-to-ceiling windows that looked out on the woods. Two people living in Amanda's LA home would keep bumping into each other, with no place for privacy. No bookshelves. No study. No place to entertain. It felt claustrophobic. I couldn't imagine spending more than a weekend there without feeling like I was in a resort, not a home.

I looked at my watch. "Hey, it's almost three. I need to get back. Batting practice starts at four thirty."

She made a sad face. "Can you come back tonight? I can't wait to have you sleep in my bed. Too bad we didn't have time to test it this afternoon."

11

———

I was restless and moody when the team flew back to Boston after our West Coast swing. There was a buzzing in my brain like an insect boring into a tree trunk. In nature, an insect infestation can sap life from a tree until it dies. I feared the insect—the emotional distance between Amanda and me— was sapping the life from our marriage.

Our marriage was a sailboat adrift in a gale with no harbor in sight. We were living apart, seeing each other sporadically, pursuing unrelated careers, and having few mutual interests. No children, no circle of friends, no plans for our future except scheduling occasional reunions. There was no "glue" in our marriage.

I couldn't imagine living in LA. The City of Angels was jarring—too many people squished into cramped developments and commuting long hours on congested freeways, with few quiet places to soothe the soul. In LA, I'd been left with the sense of being either hustled or ignored by people. I could never be happy there.

Boston and Wellesley weren't perfect, but I was embracing the East Coast lifestyle, New England's colonial history, and

Boston's art galleries, museums, and world-class universities. I even enjoyed four distinct seasons: rainy springs, hot and muggy summers, colorful autumns, and snowy winters, like in North Dakota. When I had free time, I loved to wander along Cape Cod's sandy beaches and explore small towns in Maine and Vermont. I had developed friendships with teammates who had settled in the Boston area.

Amanda sensed my feelings about being more attached to Boston. She flew to Boston at the end of August before heading to Mexico for her next film. She came to a couple of games and sat with players' wives in box seats behind the dugout. We went to dinner with teammates and their wives but talked about neutral topics: the long season, off-season winter vacations, and their kids starting school. Amanda and I had little to add to the conversations.

When Amanda and I were home in Wellesley, she retreated to our home office to read scripts and talk on the phone with her LA network. I left her alone and worked in the garden, did odd jobs around the house, and built a workbench like the ones my dad and grandfather had in their garages in North Dakota.

Our lovemaking was a formality, like shaking hands with a friend you hadn't seen in a while. The spark and passion were absent. In the mornings over breakfast, I read The Boston Globe, and she read scripts. We chatted like strangers who'd met at a coffee shop before going our separate ways for the day.

When I took her to the airport to fly to Puerto Vallarta, Amanda put a positive slant on her visit. "It was fun to watch you working around the house, Max, wearing tattered jeans, an NDSU sweatshirt, and old running shoes. You looked so happy, washing windows and painting your workbench. It reminded me of your dad doing the same things when we were home."

"Thanks, honey," I said, keeping the conversation light. "No lack of jobs when you own a home."

We played safe roles, being kind but avoiding serious discussions about the growing distance in our marriage. Friendly strangers, not passionate lovers.

* * *

I went home after the baseball season to spend a week with my parents. My mother sensed something wasn't right, but she kept her thoughts to herself. The second morning, we were drinking coffee in the kitchen. I was reading newspaper and eating Mom's scrambled eggs and toast and while she prepared lunch.

In the back of my mind, I was worrying about what Amanda was doing in Mexico. We'd talked briefly the previous night. She had been tired, drained from the humidity and heat of coastal Mexico and long hours on the set. Our ten-minute conversation had ended simply: "I love you. Talk soon. Bye."

Mom broke the ice, sensing a reason for my silence. "So, Max, you're more quiet than usual. You don't seem yourself. Is something on your mind?"

She was chop-chop-chopping onions, celery, and carrots from her garden, stirring the simmering broth, and glancing over at me hiding behind the paper. Her look said, Time to talk, son. You're being moody.

I put down the paper and sighed. Mom was fifty-two and looked forty-two. She wore pressed tan slacks and a short-sleeved flowered blouse. Her auburn hair was combed back in a bun, like you'd see in a home and garden magazine.

"You've barely talked about Amanda," she said, her tone polite, as if she were talking to one of her students who sought her out to discuss problems with school, friends, or family. "You used to talk about her all the time, but you've only mentioned that she's in Mexico. Is there something going on between the two of you?"

"Yes, there is, Mom, unfortunately," I said. "Amanda and I

are, well, kinda drifting, I guess is the way to put it. No blowups, no one's angry, but things just aren't going well."

She stopped chopping vegetables, turned off the stove, refilled her coffee cup and sat down at the table across from me.

"Want to talk about it, dear?"

I was grateful for the opening. Mom and I had had many intimate conversations at the kitchen table. "We should, Mom. I've been a little distant—my fault—but you and Dad should know. I haven't talked to anyone else about this."

"We suspected something wasn't right but didn't want to pry."

The late morning sun was streaming in through the kitchen windows, warming the butter platter. Flies were buzzing outside the screen. Autumn was in the air, my favorite season. I was glad to be home.

"I'm worried about our marriage, Mom. I'm not sure where to start."

She read the emotions on my face. Moms can do this.

"Why don't you start with why you own two homes, yours on the East Coast, hers in California. You were both happy when you bought your Wellesley home. So why did Amanda buy another home in California? Isn't it odd for a young, married couple to live far apart?"

I nodded. "I know. That's when things started to drift. Our careers keep us apart: her work in LA, mine in Boston."

She smiled, knowing my statement was merely a loose strand that would unwind the whole ball of thread. "You're missing the point, dear."

"What do you mean?"

She sipped her coffee and nibbled on an oatmeal cookie she had made for my homecoming.

"Your dad and I are old-fashioned, but how long would we have stayed married if he had lived here and I'd had a home and job in Bismarck or Minot?"

I nodded sheepishly.

"You're two very lucky people, making piles of money, having exciting careers, but you're not together more than a few weeks a year. Certainly not during the baseball season or when she's off in London or Mexico shooting a movie. How long can you keep this up?"

Bless her heart, my mother had struck a nerve.

"It doesn't look good, does it?"

She jabbed the nerve again to make sure I got her point. "Max, you haven't been happy since you bought your home in Wellesley. What happened after that?"

"Nothing you can put your finger on, but we drifted after that. We didn't talk on the phone as much, and when we did, it was mostly about our careers, not our marriage. We were both on the road most of the time. Months passed, we couldn't plan times to get together, and sometimes on the phone, we were critical of each other. Little digs, nothing really bad, but almost every conversation ended with one of us upset. Then she surprised me; she threw me a curve when she announced she wanted to buy a home in LA. I was really shocked but knew we'd have a serious argument if I didn't go along with her."

"I'm sorry, but not surprised. I sensed the same when you called and told us. Your dad and I were both shocked as well."

"I'm sure I didn't hide it well. We used to be on the same wavelength, knowing what the other was thinking, finishing each other's sentences. Now it's like we're strangers. Know what I mean?"

"I do. Most of our friends have had problems in their marriages. One or two divorced, but that brings regret and heartache that last for years. And everyone is wounded, especially the children. Most couples stay together for the kids, making compromises and sticking it out. Others struggle through a lifeless marriage, with little affection and constant tension. Having a wedding doesn't mean you'll live happily ever after."

"But you and Dad never had problems."

She smiled, like I had said something banal. "Not that you knew about, Max. We talked things out after you'd gone to bed. We had arguments, but we made compromises, knowing divorce didn't solve anything. We stayed committed. Our marriage became stronger. Being married means you compromise; you think of your spouse's needs, not just your own. Selfishness kills more marriages than infidelity. Believe me, I had to learn to do things differently so I wouldn't hurt your father's feelings. He did the same for me. We hid our struggles from others and put our marriage first. It made it stronger."

Mom didn't blink or look away. She wasn't lecturing me but was sharing the realities of married life that I needed to hear. When your mother tells you the facts of life, you pay attention.

"Max, you're smart. So is Amanda. You're both talented with bright futures. You and Amanda need to get to the root of your problems before they get more serious."

"I know. I know," I said softly, loving my mother for sharing her wisdom and advice.

"Don't leave issues hanging in the air, hoping they'll get better. A marriage is a garden that has to be tended daily—watering, weeding, pruning, and showing that you want its rewards—not just when you feel like it. If you don't give it the attention it needs, your garden will wither, get overrun with weeds, or be ruined by insects or rodents. Don't let that happen; you'll regret it for a very long time."

12

It was November before Amanda returned from Mexico. We arranged to meet in LA. The talk with my mother and months of agonizing about our marriage had made me realize Amanda and I had to have a serious talk. We had avoided confronting each other about our feelings and misgivings.

I flew to LA two days before Amanda arrived and stayed at her bungalow. When I unlocked the door and walked around, it seemed even smaller and less homier than before. She had bought more modern art, added an overhead wine rack in the kitchen, and had a new duvet with more silk pillows on the bed.

Her taste in art was puzzling; hanging in her hallway was a painting with slashes of yellow and green slanted across the canvas, looking like a leaning fence. On the fireplace mantle, planted between our wedding picture and a photo of me in a Red Sox uniform, was a mushroom-shaped blob of shiny gray metal that looked like someone had melted nickels in an ingot and poured them out. Ugly.

The first night, I slept fitfully in Amanda's bed, tossing and turning, restless about reuniting after a long separation. The distance and time had not been good; our marriage was in crisis but neither of us wanted to admit it.

In the morning, I fixed coffee and sat out on the patio, soothed by the fountain gurgling and doves cooing in her orange trees. It was peaceful—except when jets flew overhead, descending into LAX. Every three minutes.

After dressing, I went outside to walk around her neighborhood, an upper-middle-class section of West Hollywood. Every home was neat and recently painted. There were basketball backboards in driveways and palms, bougainvillea, and jacaranda in front yards. Pool-cleaning trucks were parked on every street. Home additions were under way, adding second stories onto single stories, and third stories onto second stories. People were building upward, since distances between homes were barely wide enough to ride through on a bicycle.

Foreign-car dealers were doing well in West Hollywood. Cars in driveways were predominantly new models of Mercedes, Lexus, Audi, BMW, Jaguar, Subaru, Porsche, and Volvo.

One Ferrari. New. Cardinal red. A beauty.

It was a dog-friendly area. A small army of women, thin and long-legged, wearing short shorts, tank tops, baseball hats, and sunglasses, were walking Afghan hounds, Saint Bernards, English setters, German shepherds, collies, Doberman pinschers, and Rhodesian ridgebacks, all well-groomed and wearing thick collars.

No mutts, rescue dogs, or mixed breeds.

I waved at neighbors in their yards. They smiled and greeted me with "Good morning" but gave me wary glances that hinted I might be scouting the neighborhood for nefarious reasons.

I had lunch in an Italian trattoria on Sunset Boulevard: insalata mista, seafood pasta, a glass of prosecco, and gelato. The food wasn't as tasty as at my favorite Italian restaurant in Wellesley, but I wasn't going to say anything about it to Amanda.

I bought The LA Times before returning in the afternoon to read on her patio. I skimmed through the magazines and books on her nightstand: celebrity gossip, travel, local dining, and fashion. No news magazines. A stack of well-thumbed best sellers of years past, chick lit, romance, fantasy. No nonfiction.

The second day, I took a shorter walk, ate at an Indian restaurant, bought the Times, and returned to the bungalow. I kept checking my watch as the time ticked toward 3:30 p.m., when her plane was scheduled to arrive. Amanda was taking a taxi from LAX, saving me a torturous drive on the traffic-clogged 405.

At 5:17, I heard the door unlock and hurried to greet her. The door swung open. Amanda grinned and set down her luggage. We hugged.

"Oh, Max, I'm so happy to see you," she said breathlessly. "I've missed you so much, I can't even tell you!"

"Hi, honey. Welcome home."

We kissed, but a fire wasn't smoldering. We both seemed too nervous to dash into the bedroom for a reunion session of lovemaking. Later.

Instead, we walked hand in hand into the kitchen. She chatted nervously about her flight, which had been bumpy, upsetting her stomach. I told her about my walking tour of her neighborhood and the folks who'd waved but didn't know me.

"You too?" she said with a quick laugh. "They don't recognize me either. I haven't been around much. And they don't seem to have housewarmings for new neighbors, either; only one nice woman came over when she saw a furniture truck show up. That was months ago; I haven't seen her since."

"That's LA. Everyone's busy chasing careers, raising families, and taking care of their homes. But landscapers and pool cleaners are doing well; every home seems to have a pool and a well-maintained yard."

Banal, sure. We both sensed we had to be kind to each other and not get into anything too early and spoil our reunion.

"Honey, let's go out for dinner," she said, reaching into her fridge for a bottle of water, which she drank while holding the door open, letting the cool air flow over her body. "It was dreadfully hot in Mexico. I got sick and didn't recover until last week. Some intestinal bug, then headaches, nausea, aching muscles. Everyone got it. We kept the infirmary busy and took all sorts of medicine, but nothing seemed to work except time. We were a pretty miserable bunch the whole time. But somehow we managed to shoot a movie. So glad it's over. Editing has their work cut out for them; we had lots of interruptions."

"I'm sorry," I said, reaching over to run my hand down her side, feeling ribs through her blouse. "You've lost weight, honey. Your face is thinner. And you look tired. Are you sure you want to go out? I could buy groceries and fix something here."

"No, let's not. Of all things, I want Thai food—rice, noodles, something spicy. A good wine, even. Hot tea and one of those gingery cookies for dessert. I was thinking about having a nice dinner with you the whole flight. Do you mind?"

"No, of course not."

"Good. Let me change and freshen up. I'll be fine after a shower."

"Sure. Take your time."

"I know a nice place on Beverly Drive not far from here. Then I want to come home and go to bed. I haven't slept well. The weather was blazing during the day when we were shooting, and hot and sticky at night. I don't like the tropics. Give me good old California weather with cool morning breezes."

She showered and changed into slacks and a long-sleeved blouse. I drove to the restaurant. She complained about the ordeals of shooting a movie in the tropics and all the delays with weather, illnesses, and traveling over mountain roads.

After we ordered dinner and were sipping our Pinot Grigio, Amanda's energy perked up. She reached across the table and squeezed my hand. "Thanks for being at the house, Max. I'm so glad to see you. It's been ages since Boston. Can you stay a couple weeks? I've just got this feeling that, you know, we're not seeing enough of each other. I'm worried about us."

"I feel the same way, honey. We need to stop everything and spend time together."

She squeezed my hand. "Thanks. I knew I could count on you." She sipped her wine and leaned back to relax, looking more like the Amanda I knew, not the harried, tired wife who had just survived a long flight after a stressful shooting. She looked at me, her eyes studying my face like she wanted to read my thoughts.

She cleared her throat nervously. "Are we, you know, I mean, growing apart?"

I held her look, taking a few seconds before we started round one of the serious talk we needed to have.

"I'm afraid so," I said calmly, my knees shaking under the table. "Everything changed so fast. Our lives seem to be pulling us apart. And I don't know what to do."

Her lips quivered like she was about to cry. She turned to the wall, not wanting anyone to see she was having a difficult moment. When she turned back to look at me, her voice choked. "What can we do?"

She reached up to wipe away a tear, looking to the wall again. Her breathing quickened, and a vein in her neck was pulsing rapidly.

I reached over and squeezed her wrist. She looked down at my hand and then covered it with hers.

"I'm afraid. How did we get here?" She kept her eyes down.

"You've made a wonderful life here, Amanda." My voice was trembling. This was hard for both of us, but we had to keep talking. "You have a beautiful home, good neighborhood, new friends, a busy career. I'm amazed at what you've accomplished in the last few years. I'm proud of you. You've done what many women try to do, but you made it. Big time."

She looked up at me, wiping away another tear. "Thank you, Max. I do have a nice life here, better than I ever dreamed. I've been lucky, marrying a wonderful guy like you. Having a good agent who gets me great roles. Buying a home that I love. I wish I could be here to enjoy it more. And you've been supportive the whole time, even when I wanted to buy my place. I hope you'll come to like it as much as I do."

I didn't want to comment on her home. We needed to talk about our marriage, not her bungalow. "It's easy to see you're happier here, more than in Wellesley."

When I mentioned Wellesley, she became uncomfortable. She glanced around. The restaurant wasn't busy, and we were tucked in corner away from others. She lifted her hand from mine, rubbed her fingers along her temple as if she was trying to find the right words to express her feelings. I waited for her to speak, not wanting to interrupt her thoughts.

She looked at me for a few seconds and then looked away. "I know, it may seem strange to you, but LA is where I belong. I'm sorry; I don't want to hurt you. I'm just being honest."

We were crossing over the minefield of our marriage, expressing selfish, personal desires that were driving us apart. Thoughts and feelings we'd kept from each other were coming out, words that could hurt the other. We were exposing the distance we had reached in eight years of marriage.

I swirled the wine in my glass and took a deep breath. "So here it is, as simply as I can put it: We own homes in Wellesley and LA. We have careers taking us in different directions. We lead separate lives in two cities separated by a country. It's not just the geographic distance. There's a chasm between us. It's deep — and wide."

The lines in her face tightened. Her lips were pressed

together, chin quivering, like she was about to cry. We'd reached an impasse, and no one was walking back.

"You're right, Max," she said softly, looking down at her hands. "You usually are. I feel the same, but I don't know what to do."

"We're different people than when we met at NDSU. We were young then, full of dreams, chasing exciting careers in the fast lane. We're there now, but we've paid a price to realize those dreams. There's distance between us. We don't have the 'glue' we had before—little rituals that keep us together, an invisible rope we both cling to, knowing our partner is at the other end."

I was hoping Amanda would make affirming reassurances that we were still emotionally connected and I was making too much about the distance between us.

But she didn't. She nodded, agreeing by her silence. We were quiet for a few minutes, looking aside, picking at our food, not sure what would be the right thing to say.

Finally, she stammered, "I—I'm sorry, Max. I feel the same way. We've drifted apart. I feel so bad. I don't know what we should do. Everything was going so well for us, and then, the last year, the 'glue' wasn't there anymore."

The waitress came with our dinner and noticed we were engrossed in a serious conversation. She set the plates in front of us and left us alone.

Amanda picked up her fork, swirled it around in the steaming noodles, took a small bite, and looked at me. "Are there other people involved, Max?" she asked, a tremble in her voice. "Forgive me; I don't want to accuse you of anything. It's just that I worry that being away so much, things happen. I see it all the time. I'm sorry."

I was shocked. Why would she wonder about that? It was an insult to imply that I would even think about being with another woman. Didn't she know me better than that, after eight years of marriage?

"No. Never," I said, angry that she would hint at this. "I wouldn't think about it. You know me better than that."

Her words had been like a knife stabbing my heart. I was hurt and angry, so much so that I wanted to say something critical, but held back. The chasm in our marriage had widened.

She sighed. "I'm sorry. I shouldn't have said that. Please forgive me. I know you'd never betray me."

I could forgive, but it would take time to forget.

"If no one is involved, why aren't we getting along better?"

She stirred her food and took small bites. We ate in silence, just nibbling. The food was tasteless; my emotions had done something to my taste buds. I had been hungry driving to the restaurant, but my appetite was gone. We sipped water and wine and continued to take small bites. No talking. We were both uneasy, as if we were at the bedside of a terminal patient, waiting for the doctor to announce that the patient had expired.

I put down my fork and said, "We don't have a marriage. We have two careers in two cities three thousand miles apart."

"And both traveling too much," she added. "That's a big factor. We aren't involved on a daily basis. It's like we're becoming strangers. It's so sad. I love you but don't see you. There's a wall between us—and I don't know how to get over it."

"If I thought we could make our marriage work, I'd do anything," I said, my voice cracking. "But you need to follow your career. You have talent, and LA is the best place for you to fulfill your dreams."

She put down her fork and looked at me, her face flushed, mouth downturned. "Max, before we go any further, we should see a marriage counselor."

I nodded. "Okay. That sounds good."

"I, ah, confided to a girlfriend that something wasn't working in our marriage. She recommended we see the marriage counselor that she and her husband went to. What do you think?"

"Yes. Soon. Otherwise, we'll talk in circles and not get anyplace. We need someone to help us save our marriage; we can't do it ourselves."

13

We went to see Ben, a marriage and family counselor whose Beverly Hills office was in a complex with doctors' and psychologists' offices. The walk from the street passed through a landscaped plot of flagstones, cactus, and various succulents. No shrubbery, no flowers. Subdued and tasteful.

Ben shared his office with another therapist. The waiting room had comfortable chairs, a sofa, tables with health and nutrition magazines, a coffee machine, and a bottled water dispenser. A couple sat across from us, the man feverishly paging through a magazine while his wife or girlfriend stared blankly across the room, arms folded across her chest, crossing and uncrossing her legs like it was painful being in the same room with him.

Amanda and I sat on a sofa, leafed through magazines, and listened to a clock ticking on the wall behind us. A door opened down a hallway and a young woman wearing sunglasses and a head scarf came into the waiting room and headed for the door.

A moment later a tall, husky man with red hair and a neatly trimmed beard came into view. He nodded to us, "Max, Amanda?"

We got up and followed him down a hallway with three doors: one was shut, another was a unisex bathroom, and the third was open at the end of the hall. Colored prints of nature scenes were on the walls: a Hawaiian beach, El Capitan in Yosemite, and an aerial view of an island, possibly Santa Catalina.

Ben stood outside his door and gestured for us to enter. The room was like a home office in a comfortable suburban home, with three soft leather chairs around a coffee table and a larger chair where Ben sat. On the low table were unopened water bottles, a planter with a barrel cactus, and a box of tissues.

A desk tucked in a corner was covered with papers, books, and files. Above the desk were shelves filled with books and framed family photos: a children's birthday party, a picnic on a beach, a family around a Christmas tree, and a wedding in a garden.

We sat down and Ben dispensed with an introduction. "I'd like to explain my process," he began, his voice resonant like a judge speaking from the bench. "This afternoon I'd like one of you to tell your side of the story. If it takes fifty minutes, that's fine. In the second session, I'll hear the other tell their story. In the third session, I'll give you my assessment and let you know whether I think counseling would be helpful. Who would like to begin?"

Amanda and I looked at each other, and she nodded toward me. "Max, why don't you go first."

"Okay," I said, spreading my hands in a gesture of openness. "I guess I'll start with how we met." I smiled at Amanda, remembering the cold October night nine years ago after NDSU beat UND and Debra introduced us at the kegger in the corral. I went through our first dates, my last baseball season at NDSU, the College World Series, my getting signed by the Red Sox, and our first summer on the East Coast when I started in the minor leagues and played in my first major league game in September.

Ben sat back in his large chair, hands folded across his lap, eyes looking from me to Amanda, showing no emotion. I continued chronologically with our wedding, the early years of our marriage, my career with the Red Sox, my joy about Amanda's career, and the purchase of our home in Wellesley, when everything changed. Amanda sat quietly, smiling at familiar anecdotes that I told with affection, and then looking more serious when I talked about how our marriage had drifted after buying our home in Wellesley. I choked up when I talked about how difficult the last year had been with our long separations. I concluded with memories of the good parts of our marriage, praising Amanda, and stressing I wanted to make our marriage work.

The week that followed was largely free of tension. We shopped for clothes in Santa Monica and went out to movies a couple of nights. We enjoyed dinner at a costar's home in Malibu, an evening in which all of the talk was about their movie careers and references to people I didn't know. One nice fellow made polite comments about my playing with the Red Sox, but no one else seemed to care about sports.

Amanda and I made love twice. No fireworks, just slow and familiar, sprinkled with expressions of love and caring. No everlasting words about undying commitment.

In our second session with Ben, Amanda started off by talking about her mother, her deceased father, her horrible experiences with her stepfathers, and living her teen years with her aunt's family in North Dakota. I realized that I had said little about my parents or childhood.

She gave her version of how we met that night, adding cute comments about events I'd almost forgotten. She talked about our marriage, living on the East Coast, getting some TV work, and her Hollywood career. She made brief comments about buying our Wellesley home, saying that she thought I was more attached to it than she was. She became more animated when she talked about buying her bungalow, a dream she said she'd had since she was a teenager and wanted to be an actress. She was disappointed that I wasn't open-minded and supportive of her decision to buy her West Hollywood bungalow, which she thought was not only a smart real estate investment, but also a possible future home for us.

I was surprised and a little hurt that she was critical of me for not liking her bungalow and that she felt I had not supported her career decisions. Although I didn't care for her LA home, I had always been supportive of her professional choices and successes.

No departing comments from Ben, other than, "See you next Thursday, same time."

The drive back to her bungalow in the early evening was chilly and tense. We barely spoke, and we ate carryout from a sushi place. Afterwards, Amanda went into her bedroom and shut the door. I read in the living room, watched TV until late, and went into the bedroom around one o'clock in the morning. She was asleep.

We avoided each other after that chilly evening; I worked out at a gym, took long runs in Amanda's neighborhood, and read or watched TV at night. She pleaded that she had to read scripts and meet with her agent and producers of her next movie. We ate out only once together that week; on other evenings, we ate out alone or had leftovers at home. Amanda's afternoon meetings turned into dinner invitations with her colleagues or agent. The week seemed to last a month. And it was cold and rainy. I longed to return to Boston.

We arrived at the third session fifteen minutes late. Ben was in his office and came down the hallway when he heard us entering the waiting room.

"Ben, sorry we're late," I pleaded. "Traffic's a mess, and we ran into an accident on Beverly Drive—police and ambulances blocking all streets."

He motioned for us to come down the hall to his office. His only comment: "Which means we'll have less time for this session," spoken with a hint of disappointment.

He resumed his familiar position, looked first at me, then Amanda, his face blank. We sat in silence for a few seconds, and then he began.

"I told you that today I would give you an assessment of your relationship and let you know whether or not I have hope that counseling could work for you."

He looked at me, at Amanda, and back to me, and then he continued. "I see a lot of successful people in my work. Many are like you, in busy careers with little time to spend together. Some have financial problems, addiction issues, dysfunctional families, and the stress of keeping everything going before the house of cards crumbles around them."

"We don't have those issues," Amanda replied. "No kids, no drug or alcohol issues, no financial problems. Our families aren't involved in our daily lives."

"I am very aware of that, and I consider you fortunate," he said, "more than you probably realize. You seem kindly disposed toward each other. Neither of you is carrying a lot of emotional baggage. Nonetheless, you are both clear that something is not working out between you the way you had hoped. You both have impressive careers and are making a lot of money. But you haven't communicated well this past year with all the changes in your lives. You've been avoiding intimate communication about these changes and what they mean for your marriage."

Ben paused and looked at each of us with gentle, understanding eyes. Neither one of us had anything to say; we were there to listen to him. Ben continued, "I'm sorry to say that I do not have a lot of hope for your marriage."

I held my breath and looked across at Amanda. She put a hand to her mouth, staring at Ben, not me.

"Let me explain. Please don't hesitate to interrupt me if I am not clear. I am about to say things that will not be easy to hear, so I do not offer them lightly. I offer them with concern for each of you and for your relationship. I speak the truth as I see it. But, as is often said, 'The truth will set you free, but first it will make you very uncomfortable.' Do you have any questions?

Amanda and I glanced at each other, then back at Ben. It was too difficult to look at each other for more than a moment. We were hearing a death sentence for our marriage. It was painful.

Ben continued. "One basic truth I have learned about successful people is that the attributes that makes them successful in the business world are often the causes of the breakdown in their personal relationships. That is very true about each of you."

I nodded, agreeing with him. Ben paused to let his words sink in.

"Each of you is driven to succeed in your career. You are professionally competent and disciplined, with a no-holds-barred approach to reach the top of your chosen field. You are both entertainers in an entertainment culture. If you are addicted, you may be addicted to applause. You wouldn't be the first."

I glanced at Amanda. She was nodding, her head tilted away from me.

"The reason I have so little hope for your marriage is that I perceive that each of you has made as your primary choice your career, not your marriage. You both hope the marriage will succeed, but your primary energy is for your career. There is no determined effort from either one of you to balance the two worlds."

I let out the long breath I'd been holding. I squirmed in my chair, partially out of nervousness but also because of the discomfort of recognizing the truth we were hearing.

"Neither of you—and it would actually take both of you— wants to sacrifice to make the marriage work. Or, to put it in the language of your respective careers: Max, you don't want to make a sacrificial bunt or sacrificial fly for the benefit of the team. Amanda, you want to be the star of any show, never the role that, in the old style of drama, was called fifth business.

"So, the bottom line from my perspective is that I won't schedule another session with you. I will say only that you need to make a mutual choice about the direction of your lives. Are you going to sacrifice to make your marriage work? If you mutually decide to make concerted efforts to make the marriage work, you are welcome to give me a call. I would be willing to help you at that point, but not until you have made that difficult decision."

Ben looked from me to Amanda and back again, waiting to see if either of us would respond. After a moment of silence, he said, "I take marriage very seriously. I play hardball. I would not assume to tell you what to do. I can only tell you what I can do, and I have done that."

The silence in the room was painful. Ben had accurately analyzed our marriage and diagnosed the problems. We were both at fault; our careers had driven us apart, and neither of us wanted to compromise.

Ben had his last words: "We will stop now. I will hold both of you in my thoughts with concern."

Thanksgiving and Christmas were difficult for us and our families. I spent New Year's alone in Boston. I'm not sure where Amanda was; we hadn't talked since we had boarded separate planes in North Dakota the day after Christmas.

14

———

Billy Pampas was the Red Sox left fielder: a tall, lean, handsome fellow with a haystack of blond hair that sprouted from under his cap and legs as long as fence posts.

In my favorite memory of watching Billy on defense, I was at second base when a New York Yankee slugger smacked a line drive to left center. Billy broke to his left at the crack of the bat, ran like a gazelle, snared the ball waist high, pivoted, and fired the ball to our shortstop, who tagged a runner at second base who had thought the line drive was a sure hit that would go to the wall, allowing him to score.

Fans at Fenway had groaned when the line drive had scorched toward the wall—a sure double, maybe a triple. Then the groans became screams of shock and joy. Billy got a standing ovation that lasted nearly a minute. The Yankee base runner glanced over at me as he trotted back to the dugout and muttered, "Damn, that was great play. God, he can play ball!"

The play was shown over and over on the scoreboard, was chosen to be the play of the game, and was featured on highlight reels on sports channels that night.

It was a thrill to watch Billy run in the outfield: legs moving in a blur, graceful, never stumbling, making defensive plays look so easy that an eighty-year-old grandmother could make them.

Billy was popular in the locker room—gregarious and high-spirited, like he was the happiest man in the world. Billy and I had been friends for a couple of seasons. We had long conversations about music, art, politics, and baseball on charter flights, at pregame dinners, and in the dugout.

Billy noticed I was quieter during spring training, sensing my mood had changed over the winter. But he didn't pry. He was polite and friendly, but he left me alone. He didn't confront me until the season started and we were leaving the hotel in Atlanta to go to a game.

We were the first ones on the bus to take us to the stadium. He came down the aisle where I was sitting alone near the back. He sat in the row ahead of me, turned around, and said, "Hey, Max, don't take this the wrong way, but is everything okay? You don't seem the same. How are you and Amanda?"

I held my breath, not sure what to say. I was afraid to burden anyone with my worries, and I feared gossip would spread and everyone would want to know why I wasn't making it with one of the sexiest actresses on the screen. "Aaw, well, yeah, a lot—a lot on my mind." I stammered.

"Hey, if you don't want to talk, I understand," he said. "But you don't seem like your old self. We're friends, always have been."

I was relieved that Billy had reached out to me. I did need to get out of my funk; it was a long season, and I couldn't sulk all summer. I smiled at him and patted his arm stretched over the back of his seat. "You're one of the few I can talk to, Billy. I'm sorry if I've been a little distant. Just having some problems."

Billy put his fingers to his lips when other players started boarding the bus. "Happy to talk to you anytime, buddy. Later, when we have more privacy," he said.

Later was at the end of the three-game Atlanta series; we were both at a water fountain in the Atlanta airport, waiting to fly to Chicago. A thunderstorm had delayed our flight. Teammates were wandering around, killing time in the coffee shop, and buying magazines and newspapers in the gift shop.

After getting a cool drink, we stayed nearby, our backs to the wall. No other players were around. "Max, sorry, I don't want to have you think I was being nosey before. Forgive me."

"No, no, you—you weren't nosey, Billy," I stammered again. "You were right. Amanda and I are having some problems. You know, not communicating, going through a rough patch. She bought a place in LA last year, and things haven't been the same since. And I feel rotten. Know what I mean?"

"Of course I do. You can trust me. I won't say a word."

"Thanks. I appreciate it. I haven't talked to anybody about this. I don't want it getting around."

"So you're bottling it up. Not the best way to deal with a problem, hoping others won't notice. But guys will start talking soon. Might be good to get some of it out so you're not carrying the whole burden on your shoulders."

"Yeah, you're right. How could you tell something was, you know, different?"

Billy smiled, flashing that toothy grin that was warm and disarming. He made you feel like you were the most important person in the room. He glanced to make sure no one was nearby. "We all have little secrets. I've got my own secrets I don't want anyone to know about. Nothing to be ashamed about."

"But you're the most self-effacing guy on the team. You're always cheerful. You let everything hang out. Not a care in the world."

He looked at me, his deep blue eyes shining like beacons. "I've got a whopper of a secret myself."

"Really? I never would have expected. You're always so open about everything—sex, politics, idiot coaches, lazy teammates, all the flying around we have to do during the season. Nothing seems to bother you for long."

He grinned. I felt better already, knowing I could trust Billy with my worries. "But it's a front, Max. I want everyone to think they know me so well that I could never be hiding something that scares the willies out of me."

"Could have fooled me. Everyone on the team likes you. I never hear a gripe about you from anyone."

"That's what I want. I let everything hang out. I'm talking all the time, joking around, playing the role of the happy-go-lucky guy without a care in the world."

"It works, Billy. You come across that way."

He paused and looked around the waiting lounge. No one was closer than thirty feet away. Our teammates were reading, talking, or looking out the windows as storm clouds passed over the airport. We were in a privacy bubble with no one looking at us.

Billy lowered his voice, almost to a whisper. "You'd never know I'm one of two gay guys on the team."

My head snapped around. "What?"

Billy looked around again, making sure no one could overhear. "Yup. Me and someone else you'd never guess. And I'll never tell you. Being gay in sports is a Judas kiss. All of us who love men are experienced liars; we have a secret life as gay athletes. We'd rather die than let someone know we're homosexuals. That's us: fairies, queens, homos, but also professional athletes, and some of us are damned good ones."

I was stunned. Locker room conversations were blatantly anti-homosexual, crude sometimes, even ugly. I never took part in the gay jokes, thinking a person's sexual life was private and not a subject for ridicule.

I shook my head. "I never would have guessed."

"And I can tell you, because you never got involved in the gay bashing in the locker room. You're dignified, not even using potty humor. You're classy, a true gentlemen. Otherwise I'd never have opened up to you. I know you'll keep my secret."

"Of course. I'll never say a word. Promise."

"I know you won't. I trust you. Otherwise we wouldn't be having this conversation. But I sensed something was eating you alive. I have had this radar since I was ten years old, knowing I was gay but couldn't come out. To keep my dirty little secret, I had to know what people thought of me as a boy, soon to be a man. When boys discover they're gay, it's damned scary. You play the role of being a normal, oversexed heterosexual guy so people don't get suspicious and call you out. It's a charade we all play until we're ready to leave the closet. And you can't do that in sports."

"I appreciate your confiding in me. I'll never say a word." Then I told him about Amanda and me as we stood in the waiting lounge, our backs to the wall, making sure no one else could hear us. I talked for almost half an hour, revealing my fears, loneliness, and sense of failure. I didn't hold back a thing.

Billy listened carefully, patiently, without interrupting. He heard it all: my conversations with Mom, our sessions with Ben, my sleeplessness and worry, how Amanda and I hadn't talked in weeks, and why I thought we would divorce.

When I was finished, Billy said, "Max, I'm very, very sorry about hearing this. Tell me what I can do."

"Just be my friend," I said.

When we finally got on the plane that night, I felt like a new person, fifty pounds lighter from the weight Billy had lifted from my shoulders. I slept the entire flight, the longest uninterrupted rest I'd had in months. And when I stood up to stretch after we landed, Billy was a couple of seats ahead of me. He turned around, winked, and gave me a thumbs-up. I smiled at him, a big silly grin, and gave him two thumbs-up.

Over the season, whenever Amanda and I talked, Billy was the first person I sought out to share the news. He listened, affirmed my feelings, and never offered a critical word or judgment. I always felt relieved after those talks. I knew I could make it and start a new life without Amanda.

On the field, I was having a good, almost great, season, batting .297 in June, scratching out hits, stealing bases, scoring in almost every game, and ranking high in scoring in the American League. I was in prime physical condition. My worries weren't affecting my playing. I improved as the season dragged on. I felt more confident. Billy was watching every play, cheering me when I came into the dugout after scoring, and bragging about me in the locker room. Eventually I resumed being my old self, thanks to Billy. It made a world of difference that someone else knew my story.

Billy and I were able to find a few minutes of privacy almost every day, before games, at the hotel, or between shagging flies in the outfield while other players were out of earshot. Sometimes just a few comforting words, but enough to let me know that Billy would be there for me. He told me about how gay players survived in the macho world of sports.

One afternoon, we were in the outfield, shagging flies as batters took turns in the batting cage. "As far as I know, almost every team has one or two gay players who haven't come out. We belong to this secret fraternity: not naming names, sharing our secrets, giving a knowing wave or smile when we see each other during games or warm-ups."

"But, Billy, you go out with some of the classiest women. I see you with Charlene whenever we're home. And in Chicago or Miami, there's usually a gorgeous woman waiting for you. No one would ever suspect."

A high pop-up came our way; Billy took three steps to his right, lifted his glove, and let it smack into the leather as if it was an apple falling from a tree. He tossed the ball into the infield, where it bounced twice and then rolled within inches of the pitcher's mound. He grinned as he walked back to me. "God, I love baseball, Max. Can you imagine being paid like bankers for hitting a ball or catching a fly on a sunny afternoon? I'd be miserable if I was stuck in an office every day—same desk, same phone, same computer. How did we get so lucky?"

I grinned. "You're right, Billy. We're very lucky."

Billy and I had become best friends. We talked on the phone often. I shared personal details about Amanda and me, and I kept his secret. I met Charlene, his Boston 'girlfriend,' who wouldn't tell me her last name so I wouldn't know the name of her gay brother, who played for another team. They were kind and sweet to me. One night when the three of us were at dinner, Charlene took my side in the story about Amanda.

"Max, I can't believe Amanda would be so foolish as to let you get away. She's an okay actress, pretty and funny, but directors who make romantic comedies are always on the lookout for newer, younger actresses. One day, those roles will go to actresses years younger and cuter than she is. Her time will come. I don't think she has the talent to be a character actress, like Meryl Streep or Shirley MacLaine, who played love interests in their early movies but now get roles as mothers, aunts, and divorcees. They have real acting chops—not here today, gone tomorrow starlets. When that day comes, Amanda could be a lonely, sad woman, washed up at forty."

Billy and Charlene became my saviors that season. They helped me to cope with my marital separation and to look ahead. What a difference it made to have friends who supported and counseled me during those months when I felt like a failure at marriage. By the end of the season, I could face the inevitable future: Amanda and I were going to divorce.

15

NDSU had invited former baseball teams to homecoming for the dedication of a new baseball stadium and athletic dorm. I was featured as a guest of honor and selected to be on the reunion committee.

I walked around campus the afternoon I arrived, amazed at how young the students looked—shiny faced, eyes bright with dreams about the world ahead of them, carefree in the warm cocoon that college provides. But one day they would leave campus and enter the maze of twists, turns, and dead ends they'd encounter in the real world.

I had no complaints. I had enjoyed a decent baseball career for nine years, had made good money, and felt confident about my future. There was one painful exception to my optimism: the disintegration of our marriage.

It was a bright autumn afternoon. Fallen leaves carpeted the quad in patches of orange, red, and yellow. I stopped by the business school and said hello to my former professors. They were happy to see me and praised me for my fame and financial success.

I walked the length of the campus, from the memorial

union to the undergraduate dorms and the football stadium. I was proud to be an alum and pleased that NDSU had added new classrooms and dorms, as well as a new baseball stadium.

I followed behind crowds of boisterous students hurrying between classes. Most wore jeans, running shoes, ball caps, and college sweatshirts. Some students stared at me, probably taking me for a grad student in my camel blazer, blue dress shirt, and Italian loafers. My short haircut and clean shave set me apart from the male students with their long hair, grungy jeans, and bushy facial hair.

After I returned to the quad, I passed by the fountain on my way to the memorial union for a reception with my teammates. I heard someone call out my name.

"Max! Ooh, Max, wait up!" I turned around and saw a pretty woman running toward me. She wore a navy pantsuit, low-heeled dress shoes, and a double-strand pearl necklace. I recognized Debra immediately from the smile that had greeted me every morning in class.

"Debra!" I shouted as she ran into my arms and hugged me. She looked terrific: stylish and vibrant, her short brown hair streaked with blonde and swept back on the sides. Her perfume was heavenly, like spring flowers.

"Am I ever glad to see you!" she squealed like a sorority girl, kissing me on the cheek. "I'm soooo glad you came for homecoming!"

I kissed her forehead and she giggled.

"You look great, Deb!"

"You too, big guy. Handsome as ever. You look rich and famous!" she laughed. "And you are!"

"Come on, Deb. I'm still the same old guy you helped get through marketing class."

"Yeah, and how is that helping you?" She laughed again, her eyes sparkling like morning sunlight. "As long as you're hitting the ball and scoring, you're golden. You put up some serious numbers this year. Congratulations."

I was so happy to see her. My mood soared. I felt like I was twenty years old again.

"It took me a couple of years, but it felt good."

"You kidding me? You were an All-Star! I bragged about you all summer."

"Thanks, Deb. You were always one of my greatest fans."

She clenched her fist and held it up. "I check the sports page every day to read your stats, looking for Mad Max, my old buddy. I tell everyone I helped you get an A in marketing class. I'm still waiting for tickets to a game. How about next year?"

"A deal. When and where? I'll get you four behind the dugout so you can take your friends."

"How about your home opener next year? I'll fly to Boston and bring my girlfriends."

"That's a deal. Just need your address."

She reached into her handbag, removed a small leather holder, pulled out a business card, and handed it to me.

"Any chance I can meet Billy Pampas? God, isn't he the coolest! I love that shaggy blond hair and the way he glides across the field like his feet barely touch ground. He's a dream! Is he married, by the way?"

I chuckled. "No, Billy isn't married. He's got a steady girl though."

"Damn, I'd love to swoon and flutter my eyes at him. Think he'd fall for that?"

"Go ahead. It might work. He's a good friend. I'll make sure you meet him."

She pumped her fists in the air like I remembered her doing when she was excited. "That would be so cool! I'm coming to see you play, but it'd be great to meet Billy too."

I looked at her business card. "Senior account manager with Procter & Gamble. Congratulations."

Debra cocked her head and stuck her thumbs in her blouse, sticking out her breasts.

"Not bad for a former golf jock, huh? I got promoted and assigned to the new product line we're bringing out in Europe. I'll spend the summer in Paris, Milan, and London. What do you think of that, me hanging around with famous designers? Hey, where are you going?"

"To the union for a reception for the team."

"Can I tag along? I'm on my way to see an old professor."

"Sure, let's go." She slipped her arm in mine, and we walked through the leaves, giggling and telling each other how good it was to see each other again.

Deb bubbled with joy, radiating confidence. We exchanged small talk about being back on campus, when we had flown in, our hotels, and friends we were going to see. When we got to the memorial union, she said, "What are you doing after the banquet tonight? Want to grab a drink afterwards and talk over old times?"

"I'd love to."

"I've got a sexy new dress to wear tonight. It will shock everyone who remembers when I wore only Chicago sports jerseys and sweatshirts. You can whistle at me if you like; I won't mind."

* * *

I was seated at the front table with university dignitaries and alums who had careers in professional sports and the Olympics. When I was introduced, the TV screen showed highlights of the College World Series, my playing with the Red Sox, and my hitting a home run in the All-Star game. I got a round of cheers and applause from the crowd and felt proud.

Debra met me after the awards dinner, and we walked across campus to the University Avenue hotel where both of us were staying. We ducked into the bar. After we got our drinks and found a table in a dark corner, she popped the question.

"So, Max, tell me gossip about Hollywood. I've seen a couple of Amanda's movies. My favorite is the comedy on a cruise ship when she pushed her boyfriend off the diving board and his swimsuit ripped. I laughed my head off."

I moved my drink around the table, avoiding looking at her. I praised her sexy new dress, which had gotten many stares and smiles from the alums. It was a black, silky little item with a low front and spaghetti straps. She had accessorized it with a strand of black pearls and matching earrings. She looked ravishing; every man at her table had vied for her attention after the banquet. She had seen me coming through the crowd and had weaved her way toward me.

"Sorry, boys. I've got a drink date with my old friend Max."

She had taken my arm and smiled back at the men over her shoulder.

"Baseball stars have all the luck," one of them had said.

Deb poked my arm. "I asked you: What's the latest in Hollywood?"

I shrugged and tried to sound nonchalant. "Well, I'm not really part of that scene. Amanda's career is going great, but we're kinda having some problems. We're taking a trial separation."

Deb recoiled and put a hand to her mouth. Her eyes widened in shock. "No! What happened? You're a dream couple! Famous ballplayer and actress wife."

"That's what the newspapers say, but the last year or so, we haven't been together much."

"I'm sorry. I don't mean to pry, but what happened? Sorry, I don't mean to be a pest. Tell me if it's none of my business, and I'll go away."

I smiled. Her manner was upbeat and honest, just what I needed. I'd been moody and withdrawn and was tired of it. I needed to share my thoughts with someone I trusted. Debra made that easy.

"No, I can talk to you. You know our history. If it weren't for you, we wouldn't have gotten together."

Deb moved back a few inches so she could see me better. She hadn't touched her drink since the first sip. "You two were meant for each other. You're both dynamic, attractive, and, well, fun. I like you both. I was just there to get things going. But, oh, man, I can't believe what you're telling me. I'm shocked." Deb wasn't faking it. She was obviously sincere.

"I can't believe it either. We tried counseling, but it only showed that we'd grown apart. We both travel too much. It's hard to keep a marriage together if you don't live together."

"Long-distance romances are difficult," she said, taking another sip, her eyes on me. "But you two, there was such good chemistry. You belong together. Damn, I hate to hear this. I feel like I want to cry."

Up to that point, I had shared details about my personal life with few people, but I trusted Debra. Amanda and I had occasionally wondered how she was doing after graduation.

I shrugged, a gesture of resignation. "People change, Deb. Careers can send you in different directions. After you've been married a few years and are spending most of your time in demanding careers away from each other, it's easy to drift apart. Neither of us wants to give up the careers we've built. The more we talked in counseling, the more it became clear that we were veering in opposite directions with no way to make major changes."

Deb's smile was gone She fingered her necklace, looking over at the noisy crowd watching a football game on TV at the bar.

"Max, this doesn't sound like you. You sound philosophical, almost aloof, like you're telling me about a friend and not you. But I see pain in your eyes, like you're defeated. Did you give up? Did Amanda? Are you willing to make compromises and save your marriage? Or are you both going to do nothing and watch your marriage go up in smoke? That doesn't sound like the Max I know. You've always been a fierce competitor; that's why you got where you are today, a major league star." Her voice rose as she became more angry. "Are you giving up? Tell me you're not."

It felt like Deb had lovingly slapped my face to get my attention. She had put my frustration in terms better than Ben had.

I twirled my drink in my hands and looked at her, feeling like I'd been scolded for running my bike through the mud and splashing a girl's dress.

"Thank you for that." I reached over and took her hand. "You expressed it better than I ever did."

She squeezed my hand, and we left our hands on the table next to our drinks. "Don't beat yourself up, Max. It's not all your fault. When people break up, they usually share responsibility fifty-fifty. Besides, you've got too much to offer a woman. If Amanda lets you go, she'll be sorry one day for letting such a great guy get away. Good men are a rare type, like, like an albino cheetah."

I looked at her. "Cheetah. I never thought I was a cheetah."

She grinned, teasing me. "I was stretching, trying to find some wild creature that you remind me of. Want me to make you an albino chimpanzee? How about a howler monkey?"

We both laughed, enjoying the comedic break. "No, I like the cheetah."

"Go with it, then, but, you know, I kind of like thinking of you as a howler monkey. Ever hear them screaming in the trees in one of those nature shows? They're hilarious, howling and leaping from branch to branch, pounding on their chests to show they're tough. I saw one of those shows recently, and guess who I thought about?"

Again we roared, this time with our hands squeezing, faking

little howling noises, which got us stares from the crowd at the bar. She waved at them, uttered monkey howls, and we doubled over in laughter. I hadn't had such fun in months.

We left the bar hand in hand. I walked her to her room and gave her a peck on the cheek.

"G'night, big guy. Enjoyed being with you tonight. You were a good date. Thanks." She reached up and kissed my cheek.

I walked down the hall, a little woozy from fatigue and drinks in the bar. But I was chuckling and making little monkey noises when I got in the elevator to go to my room.

* * *

The next morning, Deb and I met for breakfast, during which we chatted about all sorts of things except Amanda.

"My parents just celebrated their thirty-fifth anniversary. They're the happiest people I know," Deb said. "My dad teases Mom all the time. She buys him silly golf toys, and he makes a big fuss. They don't have a lot of money; money can't buy what they have. They act like goofy teenagers sometimes; it's so embarrassing! They even have pet names. He calls her Lucy, after the Charlie Brown cartoon, and she calls him Linus. I pray that I find someone who will make me as happy as they are."

"So, how is your love life, Deb? I'll bet you've got a string of guys chasing you."

She rolled her eyes and made a sour face. "Yeah, I had that at one time. My life's a soap opera, lots of drama with a cast of hundreds. I've dated guys who had what every girl wants, good career, smarts, attractive, but it's not enough. I almost got married a couple years ago but broke it off. I had a soul-search weekend with girlfriends and confessed he wasn't the right guy for me. I needed their encouragement to break up with him."

"What was missing?"

"We had a great time. Lots of laughs and fun times. But he wasn't my best friend. I need that—not just someone I can jump in the sack with for cheap thrills. I want more than sex; I can get that anytime. I want a guy I can wake up in the middle of the night and tell him about the wild dream I just had. I want a guy who will walk with me in the park and listen to my silly stories. I want a guy who will buy me a puppy if I ask for one. I want a guy who will always be there for me, not just during the good times. Know what I mean?"

16

I invited Deb to our opening series the next April. I picked her up at her hotel and drove her out to Wellesley to see my home. She loved it and gushed over the contemporary furniture, hardwood floors, natural lighting, and my study, where I had photos and awards from my baseball career.

I drove her back to her hotel in time for her to freshen up for our night game. We lost against the Tigers and then went out to dinner with Billy Pampas and Charlene. Deb swooned at Billy, who wore a gray Italian suit, thin tie, and pale blue shirt. He was tan from spring training. Charlene was stunning, wearing a shapely gold dress, stiletto heels, and a double strand of pearls.

Deb sat next to Billy. She teased him about his blond hair, his youthful face, and goofy sense of humor. He laughed at her silly stories, acting like they were old friends. She charmed him, and after dinner, he hugged her and told her he hoped to see her again when she was in town. We said goodbye, and I walked her back to her hotel.

"What a fun night, Max. I can't wait to tell my girlfriends! I sat with Billy Pampas and he hugged me! Said I was cute as a puppy. He's so cool, but you're right; he's not for me. Too pretty, too sexy. I don't think I'd trust him anytime I left the room. He's classy, but I need a guy who's a little homelier, devoted to me, and not checking himself in the mirror twenty times a day."

"It didn't come up, but Billy's also an artist. He paints water-color landscapes—pretty darn good ones. Maybe next time we can go to his apartment and you can see for yourself."

"Are he and Charlene, you know, hooked up? They act like good friends, but not lovers. She's really pretty and smart. I saw her look at you a few times; I think she likes you. You were having a really deep conversation there."

"Naw, we're just good friends. We hang out after games and have the same interests: art, music, books. She and Billy have been great friends. They helped me a lot after Amanda and I broke up."

"You need friends to help you get back on track. You can't do it yourself."

"So true, Deb. So true."

* * *

The season started well for me. It had been several months since Amanda and I had separated. Billy and Charlene had adopted me, cheering me up and telling me I'd be all right. The dark moods of the previous year were behind me.

I was a seasoned veteran, according to management and sportswriters. Younger players in spring training had sought me out for tips about fielding, the fierce competition, hitting major league pitching, and staying in shape during the off-season. I was generous with my advice and happy to mentor them. A few would make it; the others would get close but never fulfill their dreams.

The newspapers were after me all the time, asking about our separation and Amanda's career. I didn't want our marriage to be trivialized, so I politely deferred, "I appreciate your concern, but it's a private matter that I'd just as soon not talk about. Can we stick with baseball, please?"

After a few attempts to probe, reporters gave up, not even bringing it up off the record. Word got around, and other players and management backed me up.

Amanda's public relations person used the same approach; the celebrity media gave our relationship full coverage and then went on to the next scandal or breakup. The celebrity trades are piranhas, biting at everything that looks like a juicy story. If you stay out of their way and don't feed them anything, they'll find other targets and feast on them.

Our divorce was final in August. A couple of lines in the press, and we were history. My social life that season was with Billy and Charlene, other players, and their wives. I got invited to parties, dinners, and special events. I chose carefully, staying away from the public, preferring dinners at friends' homes. And somehow, there was always a pretty woman seated next to me—sometimes as a surprise; other times, I'd been tipped off.

I was single again, a professional baseball player, available and sought after. But I wasn't interested in dating. I just wanted to be with people I trusted. My divorce had made me shyer, and I had the feeling I was being watched, graded, and targeted. Notes were slipped to me in hotels, in restaurants, and at parties: women's names, phone numbers, e-mail addresses, and sometimes flattering photos. I dropped them in the wastebasket when I got home. Not interested.

If I wanted to date a woman, it would be someone I chose because of her personality, intelligence, attractiveness, and maturity. I wasn't in a hurry.

My confidence was coming back. I was able to concentrate on playing the best baseball I could, spending time with friends, and being alone. I needed time to think through where I was in life, and how to re-create a social life, with no pressure. I gobbled up books, mostly biographies from the nineteenth and twentieth centuries: Napoleon, Bismarck, David Lloyd George, Hitler, Churchill, FDR, Lindbergh, Stalin, and JFK.

I accepted offers to serve on foundation boards in Boston and began making generous contributions to charities involved with education, drug abuse, prison reform, and conservation.

I felt I was maturing into a more serious person and setting long-term goals. I was maintaining good physical condition, building strong relationships, giving back to the community, and planning for life after baseball. There were lots of interesting fields I could choose, but I was sure of one thing: It wouldn't be politics. I wanted distance from the spotlight.

My baseball career wouldn't last forever, and I wanted to prepare for the next chapter in my life. I had started dating again but made it clear that I was interested in friendship and good communication. One woman I saw frequently was a dynamic, divorced finance executive from New York. After a few dates, our careers interfered with how much time we could spend together. Plus, she had two preteen children, and I wasn't prepared to become a stepfather. If I was going to have children, they would be mine. We parted amicably and even continued to send nice notes to each other, but there were never hints that we should try again.

One night at a postgame dinner at Billy's, Charlene sauntered over to me and rubbed my shoulder with hers. "So, Max, have you found that lucky girl yet? Ready to get back into circulation?"

I put an arm around her and squeezed. "Charlene, trust me, you're the first person I'll tell when I'm ready."

"I know a couple of cuties you'd like. Funny, smart, good careers. Say the word, and I'll set up a date. You're quite a catch; don't become a hermit."

"I won't, Charlene. You know me better than that."

17

My early thirties were a time of turbulence and change. Somewhat naively, I had thought I would spend my baseball career in Boston and remain there after I retired. I loved living on the East Coast, with all of its historical locations, cultural events, and Cape Cod beaches, as well as the friendships I had formed.

But my contented life in Boston was swept away when general managers of major league teams were horse trading during winter meetings in Florida. I was traded to the Seattle Mariners in a complicated swap involving ten players shuffling among the Red Sox, the Chicago White Sox, and the Seattle Mariners.

The Red Sox needed to bolster their pitching roster; I was the bait in the three-team swap. Trading my services as second baseman, the Red Sox received a highly rated rookie pitcher from Chicago and a veteran reliever from Seattle. The trade made sense as a business transaction but came with personal costs to all players involved.

Being traded is a risk in professional sports. For the privilege of making hefty salaries playing a game they love, players mortgage away decisions about where they'll spend their careers. General managers make decisions in the best interests of teams, not the desires of their players. It's the real world.

Leaving Boston was a blow, personally and professionally. I'd leave close friends, especially Billy and Charlene. I would miss so many experiences that made Boston special: sailing in Boston Harbor; walking around the Boston Common and Freedom Trail; biking along the Charles River; visiting the birthplaces of John Adams, John Quincy Adams, and JFK; and little touches like drinking Sam Adams lager at pubs near Faneuil Hall Marketplace.

I would especially regret missing afternoon games at Fenway against our biggest American League rivals, the New York Yankees. Those games were some of my greatest memories.

The trade, of course, meant not living in Wellesley anymore. I didn't want to sell my home, so I decided to rent it. I had once dreamed that Amanda and I would start a family in Wellesley and watch our children grow up, play sports, go to playmates' birthday parties, and enjoy holidays in our quiet suburban home.

Amanda called me after the trade. She was cordial, wished me success with the Mariners, and inquired what I was going to do about Wellesley. I told her of my decision to rent it, resettle in Seattle, and not make any long-term decision about it for the time being. Amanda and I had talked rarely since our divorce, exclusively about careers and parents. Nothing about our personal lives. We respected each other's privacy and left it at that.

Playing for the Mariners meant I'd be in Anaheim during the season to play two three-game series against the Angels. I didn't want to see Amanda and expected that she felt the same way about me. What would be the purpose? Maybe in a few years we could see each other, after the painful memories had faded. I didn't know how Amanda felt, I just knew I didn't want to see her.

Deb also called me after the trade. We'd talked a couple of times after she'd come to Boston. She was disappointed that I'd be playing on the West Coast but said she would try to come to a game when Seattle played in New York, her busy work and travel schedule permitting. She was moving up the corporate ladder at P&G. I complimented her on her career and inquired if she had found a special guy and was ready to settle down.

"So many men, so little time," she said. "I'm juggling, tap dancing, whistling 'Yankee Doodle Dandy,' and spinning plates at the same time. Having a blast. Too busy to slow down and smell the roses. But you'll be the first I'll tell when Prince Charming shows up. You can count on it."

* * *

After spending Christmas with my parents in snowy North Dakota, I returned to Boston to pack up before flying to Seattle to find a place to live. I rented a comfortable apartment near the University of Washington in a quiet neighborhood with bars, restaurants, parks, and schools.

I flew to Phoenix in early February for my first spring training in Arizona's Cactus League. Teams in the Cactus League are predominantly from the West Coast, with a few from the Midwest.

The Mariners' spring training stadium was in Peoria, a Phoenix suburb. I'd invited Mom and Dad for my first Arizona spring training, but both were dealing with ailments, Mom with diverticulitis and Dad with a bad case of the flu.

I was anxious about joining my new team, which I imagined would be a bit like showing up for freshman orientation on campus. But my new teammates and management greeted me warmly and made the experience pleasant and hospitable. Within a couple of days, I was going to dinner with them; meeting wives, girlfriends, parents, and friends; and feeling like I'd been adopted by a large family.

My new teammates and I had a lot in common. We swapped stories of past seasons and talked about opponents we loved to beat, players on other teams we respected, the rigor of long road trips, and frustrations when our team wasn't winning. Most of all, we shared a love of the game we'd started playing as young boys in the United States, Canada, the Dominican Republic, Venezuela, Puerto Rico, and even Cuba.

I had a good spring training, but the Mariners played poorly, trying out a crop of rookies and minor leaguers who weren't ready for the big leagues. Our Cactus League opponents were power teams like the San Francisco Giants, Los Angeles Dodgers, San Diego Padres, and Arizona Diamondbacks. We lost most of our games to them.

When spring training ended and the team headed to Seattle for our home opener, I was not optimistic about the season. My concerns were affirmed; we had a disappointing season, finishing fourth in the Western Division, just above .500. Our weaknesses were many: weak pitching, an inexperienced bullpen, and an offense that failed to perform in clutch situations. Many players were not as seasoned as my former Boston teammates had been.

After the season, I considered returning to Boston, but I'd rented my Wellesley home with a two-year contract to an MIT professor. It was a good financial arrangement, but it left me without a place to live and enjoy New England's glorious autumn leaves. I stayed with Billy for a week and saw friends and former teammates, but it wasn't the same as living in my home.

I returned to Seattle and applied to take courses in computer science and marketing during the University of Washington semester break in January. I liked the discipline of being in the classroom again; students recognized me but let me have my privacy.

My best friend during the off-season was a Mariner team-mate. He and his wife lived on Bainbridge Island. We went to Seahawks and SuperSonics games, hiked and mountain biked on Bainbridge, enjoyed meals at many of Seattle's ethnic and artisan restaurants, and skied in British Columbia over the holidays. The winter went by fast, and on New Year's Day I was looking forward to spring training in warm and sunny Arizona. The rain in the Pacific Northwest will do that to you.

I showed up in Peoria about five pounds heavier than I liked. I ran sprints, lifted weights, and worked with trainers on increasing my upper-body strength. In an early game, I got hit on the elbow by a pitch. X-rays showed a bruise; I didn't play a complete game until mid-March.

I started the season wounded and played like it. I had an average season with the Mariners, hitting .277 with fifteen home runs. My confidence was waning, even my desire to continue playing baseball. Playing in Boston had spoiled me; playing in Seattle forced me to think more of my future after baseball. I remembered my talk with Rocket about the sand flowing in the hourglass of time.

If I was lucky, I would have another season or two before retiring. I was not looking forward to the day I'd hang up my spikes and join the working world. I continued taking courses in finance and computer science with no idea if those classes would help in a post-baseball career.

At the end of my third season in Seattle, I retired from professional baseball after ten seasons with the Red Sox and three with the Mariners. I was thirty-four without a job.

I spent a year in transition, not wanting to start a job search before deciding what career seemed most promising. My Wellesley home was rented out for another year, and I was satis-fied living in Seattle with its many attractions—both its natural beauty and its stimulating diversions.

Deb had been a good friend when I was making the decision

to retire. I called her several times. She was a patient listener, complimented me on my decision, and encouraged me to take time off before starting a new career. We talked about getting together, but it never quite worked out. Probably for the best; talking long distance was a comfort. Spending a weekend together might put a strain on a relationship that was evolving slowly.

I kept up a rigorous physical regimen, hiking and mountain biking in the Cascades, kayaking and sailing on Puget Sound, and playing basketball and squash at the university gym. I was determined to keep my weight stable and not balloon like some athletes after they retire.

I had more time to read, choosing mainly biographies and American history from Colonial times, the Civil War, and World Wars I and II. I read The New York Times, The Wall Street Journal, and the Seattle P-I daily. I browsed professional want ads, curious about what career would appeal to me—finance, marketing, teaching, or even coaching.

I felt waves of nostalgia when spring training began in the first February after I retired. For the first time in more than a dozen years, I wouldn't be going to Florida or Arizona to join my team. I devoured the sports pages, followed Red Sox teammates, watched games on TV, critiqued players' performances, and wondered if I might have retired too early.

I felt the urge to fly to Boston for opening day in April. On a whim, I booked a flight, thinking it would be fun to reconnect with former teammates, meet the new crop of rookies, and spend time with friends. But after mulling over the decision, I canceled the flight, not wanting to appear as another "old-timer" invading the locker room to relive past glories. I had to move on with my life.

One Sunday morning, I spotted a classified ad in the Seattle paper, a job in state law enforcement that required a government security clearance and background investigation. I cut out the ad, mailed it to Dad, and said we'd talk about it when I was home for Easter.

"Sounds like an interesting position, son," he said when we were having coffee at the kitchen table the morning after I arrived. "I never thought my son would choose law enforcement, but you'd be good."

He shuffled his coffee cup around the table while my mother prepared ham and sweet potatoes for a big Easter dinner with friends.

"What do you think, Mom?" I asked, knowing she was paying attention to our discussion.

"It's up to you, son. Our family has a long tradition of enforcing the laws. Everyone respects the work the police do. You'd make a good officer; I just hope you don't have to spend a lot of time with criminals."

Dad shook his head. "No, this agency does more investigative work. Max has a good education for that."

"Yes, that appeals to me," I said.

"Whatever you do, put your heart in it, Max," Dad said. "Every job will disappoint you at times, including this one. Don't take it home at night. Have things to occupy yourself—friends, sports, community work. Find a church and join. When the time's right, get married again. Listen to me—I sound like your mother. She thinks every man needs a wife and should belong to a church."

Mom laughed. "Dear, don't worry about that. Max will find the right woman. It takes time; he's in no rush."

I chuckled. "You're right. I have good friends in Seattle. We do fun things, mostly outdoors, and we go to museums and places like that. And I will start going to church. A good woman will show up one day. "

* * *

After I returned to Seattle, I filled out the application, which required references and names of supervisors to vouch for my character and work ethic.

For references, I listed the former president of the North Dakota Association of County Sheriffs. He was a longtime friend and hunting partner of Dad's whom I had first met when I was twelve years old and they took me on my first pheasant hunt, an annual October event.

I included my baseball coach at NDSU, the manager of the Red Sox, the commissioner of baseball, and Billy Pampas, one of the most popular players in major league baseball.

I imagined a water cooler conversation in the human resources department when they read my references. They probably didn't receive many applications with character references from prominent people in professional baseball.

I went through interviews with high-ranking officials who praised my experience, references, and education. When I received my acceptance letter, I was gratified that I'd found a career in law enforcement, maintaining a three-generation family tradition.

I began a training program with twenty men and women about my age, many who had changed careers like myself. My classmates knew about my baseball career, but after a few polite conversations, I told them I wanted to be taken seriously as a professional law enforcement officer, not a washed-up ballplayer.

Training involved classroom lectures, working in the field with professionals, field trips to the headquarters of the Highway Patrol, the county sheriff, the Seattle police, the FBI, and a small Secret Service detachment.

After graduation, I was assigned to a team coordinating investigations with state and federal law enforcement involving white-collar crime, money laundering, cybercrime, and securities fraud. My badge said Lieutenant, Washington State Department of Law Enforcement.

My social life was pleasant but sporadic. I dated a lawyer, a teacher, an author, an artist, and a filmmaker I'd met at functions at the university. These women were smart, ambitious, and career-oriented. They enjoyed the same outdoor sports as I did, so we spent many weekends in the Cascades, in Whistler, and on Mount Rainier.

Another anniversary of my divorce from Amanda came and went. I didn't realize it until a week later. A good sign—my life was focused on my new career and social life.

It didn't bother me anymore when I read about Amanda's movies. She was appearing in two movies a year, getting decent reviews, and developing a buzz as the next possible Julia, Jennifer, or Scarlett. All she needed was a breakout movie.

I was wary that Amanda might be getting in over her head with the publicity that comes with a Hollywood career. Paparazzi paired her with handsome actors at movie premieres, hyping that they were the next celebrity couple. A month later, she'd be on the arm of another eligible actor at a premiere or vacationing in Thailand, Hawaii, or the Caribbean.

Being a much-photographed celebrity can warp one's judgment. I'd seen it with ballplayers who thought they could bend the rules because they were famous. Whether it was drugs, women, gambling, or arrogant behavior, bad decisions had ruined careers, reputations, and families.

I hoped Amanda would never be thrust into the harsh glare of a scandal.

18

Then it happened. It was a cool fall day, and I was drinking morning coffee in the kitchen, dressed for work, and reading the Seattle Post-Intelligencer. A chill ran down my spine when I saw the headline in the lifestyle section:

Italian Director Drowns in Home Swimming Pool

Three photos: a swimming pool in Bel Air encircled by police tape; a publicity shot of Italian director Damiano Sartor, Amanda's lover; and Amanda; grim faced, wearing sunglasses, hair in a tight bun, dressed in black, being escorted by her agent from Sartor's home.

The story was the plot of a cheesy B-grade Hollywood movie about the lives of the spoiled and semi-famous. Sartor, a roguish Italian director, had been found floating facedown in his pool by a maid who arrived the morning after a party Sartor had thrown at his home.

According to the article, Sartor had struck his head on the edge of the pool, had fallen in, and had drowned around 7:30 a.m. Amanda hadn't been at the party; she'd been on a movie set in Burbank.

The media swarmed over the scandal like vultures picking over a carcass, reporting juicy details about the party's guests from Hollywood's central casting: long-legged, sultry actresses, pretty-boy actors, shady directors, and bit players in low-budget cable movies lusting for career breaks by hanging around Sartor and his sleazy friends.

Not the types you'd see at a church picnic or ice cream social.

Subsequent stories reported rumors that Sartor and Amanda had been going through a rough patch in their six-month relationship. Sartor had invited a young Italian actress who'd recently arrived in Hollywood to join him on a yacht off Cabo San Lucas. Paparazzi had photos of the actress sunbathing topless on the deck, Sartor handing her a drink. Their bathing suits were the size of dinner napkins.

Sartor and Amanda had argued in a Santa Monica restaurant the week after the yachting story. She had stormed out, and the paparazzi had photographed her speeding out of the parking lot and almost running down a valet.

The story was front-page news for a week in the scandal rags and the lead in celebrity gossip cable shows. There were numerous photos of the pool with arrows pointing to where Sartor had hit his head and fallen in. Reporters quoted "unnamed sources" who said guests had stayed late, drunk heavily and taken drugs. One actress had dove naked into the pool.

Amanda was questioned by the police, as were all guests. Everyone denied drug use and praised Sartor as a "genius and auteur." The coroner concluded that the death was accidental, possibly the result of being semi-intoxicated in the early morning when he fell and hit his head.

The media camped out in front of Amanda's Montecito home, south of Santa Barbara. There was no mention of the bungalow she'd purchased when we were married. Her agent told the media that Amanda was in seclusion at the Palm Springs home of a friend and was postponing a return to the set of her latest movie, which was being shot in Burbank.

I didn't call Amanda during the scandal. It had been three years since we'd talked. She had enough stress with the sensational coverage. I was mentioned in early stories as her former husband, a footnote in the Hollywood scandal. Scandal sheet reporters contacted me, and I refused their calls.

But I remembered "our conversation."

19

I was invited back to homecoming as a new board member of NDSU's foundation. I'd be joining alums running companies in energy, technology, and pharmaceuticals who were contributing to the university's building and academic programs.

The invitation provided an opportunity to invite Deb as my guest. We had mentioned getting together a few times, but living on opposite coasts made it complicated. Meeting halfway at NDSU was a compromise.

Deb had become a lifeline during the turbulent years after the divorce, my trade to Seattle, and my decision to retire from baseball. A casual college friendship had evolved into a relationship of mutual respect and confidentiality. No hidden agendas or expectations. We just liked each other.

During a long late-night phone call, Debra had confided in me about romantic relationships she had terminated, where the ending had come as a surprise for the unlucky fellows. I asked her why she had ended those relationships.

"It's funny, Max. I see the end of an affair long before the guy does. So I end it and move on. The men involved—and they're men, not boy toys—are stunned. I let them down gently, tell them we're not right for a long-term commitment, which, of course, is what we're all looking for in life. Better to be free and find the right person."

"That takes courage," I said.

"And a lot of lonely Saturday nights. But I'd rather be by myself than with someone who won't be in my future. I have girlfriends who hang on to a guy until the bitter end, hoping things will change. But they don't. When the breakup comes, there are the usual hard feelings, nasty words, and emotional wreckage. Marriages end up worse, with courtroom battles about money, property, and custody of children. I'll never get into that situation."

That was one of the things I liked about Deb: her brutal honesty.

My heart skipped a beat when I spotted her across the room at the opening reception, surrounded by admiring male alums. It looked like she was flirting and entertaining them with bawdy stories.

She looked glamorous in a low-cut purple dress and teardrop earrings that sparkled like diamonds. Her hair had been styled in such a way that she looked like a sultry French actress.

She spotted me, waved, and excused herself. She hurried through the crowd, her smile radiating like sunrise on a beach. I opened my arms and we embraced. "I'm sooooo glad to see you, Max," she whispered in my ear. "It's been waaaay too long."

Her perfume was delicious, spicy with a hint of lime.

I kissed her cheek and ran a hand across her back. "I've missed you. Thanks for coming."

"Wouldn't miss seeing you again, hot stuff."

Our extended embrace wasn't missed by nearby alums who enviously glanced our way while they quaffed beers and cocktails.

When we separated, we held hands at our sides. "You look smashing; I love your dress."

"Oh, good! I bought it in New York, thinking 'what the hell,' let me shock some big-shot alums this weekend. I might get sued if one of them has a heart attack."

"Go for it; I'll hire a lawyer."

"You're a doll, my knight in shining armor."

We laughed, soaking up warm feelings of being together after a long time. A good start to the weekend.

"Hey, we better quit gawking at each other," she said. "Someone might tell the provost, and they'll ask us to leave."

Deb gazed around the room at the expensively dressed alums and university officials. "Is it just me, or do some of these guys look like they're getting soft?"

"Remember, we're in North Dakota. You live here, you put away a lot of prime rib and baked potatoes for the winters."

She squeezed my hand. "But not you. Handsomer than ever, big guy."

Someone rang a bell, the double doors into the dining room swung open, and the crowd headed in. We walked hand in hand and picked a table at the rear. We waved at familiar faces as old acquaintances filed past and stopped to exchange greetings. We received a couple of stares from alums who probably hadn't heard that Amanda and I had divorced.

Tuxedoed student waiters passed from table to table, pouring wine, taking orders, and welcoming us back to campus. Deb and I jabbered, hands clasped under the table. She acted like a party hostess, telling funny stories, flirting with older alums, and whispering during a boring introductory speech.

After the dinner, Debra and I headed outside for fresh air. "Let's go for a drink on University, like old times," she said. "Tons to talk about."

"Good idea. Too early to call it a night. Did you tell friends you were going to North Dakota for a wild weekend?"

She laughed. "North Dakota? Wild weekend? You mention going to North Dakota and people assume you're going pheasant hunting. But I told girlfriends you invited me. They want me to come back with juicy gossip about you. Don't disappoint me."

"I won't, promise."

I helped her put her shawl over her shoulders and took her hand as we walked in the moonlight across campus to University Avenue, commenting on how much had changed over the years. Designer clothing stores, ethnic restaurants, gourmet tea shops, and electronics stores had replaced used bookstores, smoky bars, and the foreign movie theater.

We ducked into an Italian trattoria and ordered prosecco and biscotti for a nightcap. We nestled in a back corner, listening to romantic arias from La Bohème playing softly in the background.

"Nice place," I said.

"Sure is. More romantic than the dive bars with peanut shells on the floor where we used to drink cheap beer."

Deb's perfume was more intoxicating than the prosecco. I felt good, even a little feisty.

"Those were good times, though," she added. "I wouldn't trade memories of old NDSU for anything."

"Same here. But I'm not nostalgic for the good old days; you have to keep moving forward in life, not dwell on the past."

We looked around at the art deco Italian travel posters on the walls as we sipped prosecco, our thighs touching.

Deb said, "All these Italian touches remind me of that ugly story about Amanda and the sleazy Italian who died. I felt sorry for her. Did you talk to her about it?"

"No, and didn't want to. What would I say? 'Sorry you're going out with a creep'?"

"He wasn't her type—older, shady reputation, out of her league. The magazines said it had been an on-again, off-again thing that went on too long. If she'd been my girlfriend, I'd have told her to dump the loser."

"The tabloids contacted me, looking for a juicy quote, but I had nothing to say. One even came to my apartment and said he'd flown up from LA just to talk to me. No way I wanted to get mentioned."

"Hasn't hurt her career so far. But she needs better scripts; her last movie was lame. Critics chewed it up and spit it out with a bad taste in their mouths. I don't understand how Hollywood works. They keep making movies for demographic groups: adolescent boys, dreamy-eyed teenage girls, and twenty-year-old romantics. Amanda is always cast in the same role: saucy femme fatale, attractive, with great clothes and foxy girlfriends. Guys chase her like she's the newest puppy in the yard. She gets the leading man after a lot of jokes and silly foreplay. Her agent needs to get her roles that have meat on them. No more cupcake movies; she's better than that."

"You should be in Hollywood making movies."

"Naw, I like the real world. No time for tinsel and testosterone."

"Anybody new in your life?"

She shook her head. "Not since the last one I told you about. I thought he was a contender: nice family, great job, and more ambitious than I am. We were twins: Jack and Jill Go-Getters, workaholics, traveling all the time. We arranged dates by e-mail from different time zones."

"Sounds familiar."

"I remember what you said about you and Amanda. But, silly me, I thought it would change and I'd settle down and take care of babies. He wanted to get engaged, but when I mentioned I wanted to have babies, he reacted like I'd brought a python home for a pet. His idea of a marriage was a business partnership. At a candlelight dinner, he wanted to talk about spreadsheets and financial projections. I want someone who cuddles at night and tells me how crazy he is about me."

She moved closer and slipped her arm through mine.

"Are you glad we got together this weekend, Max?"

"Absolutely. I'd been wanting to see you for quite a while."

"Me too. Did you ever imagine that we'd ever come back to old NDSU and end up late at night in a little Italian place, snuggling like bunnies, talking about past loves that didn't work out? Think that means something? Or is it just the wine?"

I put my hand under the table and placed it on her thigh, tracing my fingers over her silky dress. "What took us so long to get here?"

She purred, "I don't know or care, but we finally made it. I'm glad we did."

"Me too." I squeezed her thigh.

She tilted her head to give me a kiss on the cheek. "Did I ever tell you I give a killer back massage? Let me know when you want one. First one's a freebie."

"How about tonight?"

* * *

I missed the homecoming golf tournament the next morning after spending the night in Debra's hotel room. We made love for the first time that night and again in the morning. We skipped the afternoon lecture and took a drive along the Red River outside of Fargo.

After the banquet on Saturday night, we returned to her room. After making love, we lay under the covers, talking about how good it felt to be together. Deb rolled over, kissed me, and said, "You invited me here for the weekend. My turn now. Why don't you come to Aspen and go skiing in January? My friends have a time-share. We ski all day and then sit around a cozy fireplace and drink wine from the cellar: French Bordeaux, Italian Chianti, and Napa Cabs."

"Not a bad idea."

"I'll introduce you as an old flame I picked up on campus."

"Think anyone will believe you?"

She nuzzled her head under my chin. "I don't care what they think. I just want to be with you."

20

———

T he Western States Law Enforcement Association holds an annual conference every February featuring the latest scientific and technical equipment in the field. I had attended my first conference in Denver the previous winter and signed up for my second, held at the Las Vegas Convention Center.

I left a rainy, chilly Seattle on a Thursday night and woke up the next morning in warm, sunny Las Vegas. I registered in the lobby and went to a breakfast reception in the main conference room with a thousand other members from the Western states.

Following the opening session, I went to a panel on computer security and firewalls to prevent hackers from penetrating law enforcement servers. When I was leaving that panel session, three men approached me in the hallway wearing conference badges pinned to their sport shirts.

The shortest man, about fifty-five with thick, wire-rimmed glasses, introduced himself. His badge identified him as being with the Los Angeles Police Department.

"Mr. Bauer, my name is Hal Lamont. I'm with the LAPD. My associates are detectives Freeman and Hopgood." He gestured to the men beside him, a tall black man who looked like a former football player and a stocky, younger man with a military-style crew cut and ruddy face.

"Could we have a few minutes of your time?" Lamont said.

We shook hands, and I checked their badges. Freeman was the black man, Hopgood the ex-military type.

"Sure. What is this about?"

The low-ceilinged hallway was crowded and noisy. Attendees were making their way to panel sessions and stopping at booths where vendors were exhibiting surveillance cameras, miniature cameras and recorders, night-vision devices, video cameras for police cars, collection kits, and vehicle tracking equipment.

Lamont raised his voice to overcome the distracting noise from video presentations and demonstrations by salespeople.

"If you don't mind, we could talk more privately in another location."

"Sure. Lead the way."

I followed Lamont, Freeman, and Hopgood through the corridor, into the lobby, and down an adjacent hallway where a large room had been partitioned for smaller gatherings. Lamont opened the door to conference room B, which had a temporary sign: LAPD.

Conference room B was long and narrow, the width of the hallways. The furniture was plain and simple: a table with a white cloth in the center, eight plastic chairs on each side, and another table against the wall with a pitcher of ice water, coffee dispensers, Styrofoam cups, plastic water bottles, soft drinks, and bowls of granola bars and fresh fruit.

Lamont closed the door, went to the coffee dispenser, and poured a cup. "Please help yourself to coffee or anything else you'd like," he said. Freeman and Hopgood grabbed water bottles and waited for Lamont to sit down. When he did, they sat on either side of him.

I passed on refreshments and sat across from them.

Lamont said, "Sir, thank you for giving us a few minutes of your time. I called your supervisor yesterday and asked if we could meet you and discuss an investigation we're working on."

"He left me a message this morning. What is this about?"

Lamont nodded toward Freeman and Hopgood. "The three of us are on a team investigating the death of Damiano Sartor, your former wife's boyfriend."

"Oh, I see. Bizarre story, but all I know is what I read in the papers."

Lamont replied. "Have you by any chance talked to your former wife about the accident?"

"No, I haven't. We haven't talked much since our divorce."

"I see," Lamont said, nodding his head. "With your permission, we'd like to share with you the status of our investigation."

I was puzzled. Why would they want to talk to me about Sartor's death? "All right, I suppose."

Freeman reached into a briefcase, pulled out a bulky folder, and passed it across to me. "This is some of the material we have in the file. If you'd like, you could look through it."

I opened the folder. On top were photos of Sartor's backyard enclosed by yellow police tape: the patio, pool, ladder, diving board, cabana, lounge chairs, tables, shrubbery, trees, and garage wall.

I flipped through the photos. Several showed detritus from Sartor's party: drinking glasses, some still half full of liquids; empty liquor and wine bottles; trays of dried cheese, breads, olives, and onions; silver ice buckets; ashtrays; cigarette packages; a scarf; sunglasses; a bracelet; earrings; a wallet; and a purse with a silver chain.

Under the photos was a two-page list of people questioned about the accident; Amanda's name was at the top of the first page.

Under the list were summaries of police reports from interviews with party guests and Sartor's maid, chauffeur, and neighbors.

I scanned a few of the reports, closed the folder, and pushed it back across the table to Freeman. "I'm sorry, but I don't have time to read through this. What did you want to talk to me about?"

Lamont said, "Two things. First of all, we wanted to meet you." He smiled, the first time he had expressed any emotion. "You had quite an impressive baseball career, Mr. Bauer. I enjoyed watching you play on TV, but I have to admit we're Dodger fans. Most Angelenos are," he boasted, his smile widening.

Freeman and Hopgood also grinned, squirming in their chairs to get more comfortable. The mood in the room had become more relaxed.

"Well, thank you," I said, "and please call me Max. I loved playing baseball. But I never had the privilege of playing against the Dodgers. I'm sure we would have pounded them."

"Ha, ha, ha!" Lamont, Freeman, and Hopgood hooted, slapping the table like they were at a baseball game. For a moment, they weren't stone-faced detectives, but young boys who had grown up in LA rooting for the Dodgers. It was pleasant to share our love of baseball, an ice breaker in many conversations with men meeting for the first time and finding a common interest.

Lamont smiled and shook his head. "Not sure, Max. Depends upon the year and the team. Certainly not last year, but this year the Red Sox could probably whip the Dodgers. Especially if you were still playing for them."

We all laughed, and then the levity was over, like a candle being snuffed out.

Lamont continued, "But seriously, the second reason we wanted to meet you was to tell you that we're willing to share any information we have on the investigation."

I shrugged, still uncertain as to why they wanted to talk to me. "But what can I do? It's your investigation."

"Yes, but we'd like to ask you a few questions. You answers might help us."

I shrugged again and held up my hands in a "why me?" gesture. "I don't know what I can tell you. I haven't talked to Amanda in months."

Lamont followed quickly. "Did she call you after the accident?"

"No. And I didn't call her."

Lamont looked at Freeman and Hopgood, who nodded but didn't say anything. "Very well. I'd like to share what your former wife said when we questioned her."

"That's fine. But I don't know how I can help you."

"I'll make it brief. I know you want to get back to the conference."

"Yes, I do, but we can talk some more."

"The three of us questioned your former wife on the day of Sartor's death and a second time a few days later. She was distressed but answered our questions willingly. We asked where she'd been the night before and the morning of the accident. She said she had been in Burbank on the set of a movie she was shooting and hadn't left Burbank until her agent called to tell her about Sartor's death. She then drove to his house, where we questioned her. Later we went to Burbank to verify her story. It was just like she said; her presence was backed up by security cameras. She was staying in a studio cottage arranged by the movie company. She returned from the set around 5:30 p.m. and then left the cottage at 7:30 p.m. for dinner, returning at 9:30 by herself. She remained in her cottage until the next morning, when a car pulled up in front of her cottage. A woman got out and went into her cottage, and the two came out half an hour later and walked to the movie set. Her agent called around

11:00 a.m., and she left and drove to Sartor's home, where we met her."

"I see. I didn't know any of that. The newspapers reported that she was in Burbank that night."

"We also questioned the young woman, a Ms. Pauline Cox, who went to dinner with her that night. They ate at a Chinese restaurant and left a little after 9:00 p.m. Both returned to their homes. The restaurant confirmed their presence and provided a copy of the credit card receipt for the dinner. Your former wife paid the bill."

I nodded. "So, what's the problem? She wasn't at Sartor's home that night. She was in Burbank."

Lamont pursed his lips and frowned like a tooth was bothering him. "In a word, forensics."

"Forensics? What do you mean?"

"When detectives arrived at 8:45 a.m. at Sartor's home after his maid called 911, they sealed off the area. A forensics team arrived at 10:00 a.m. and swept the area, collecting cigarette butts, drinking glasses, cups, and plates left over from the party for fingerprinting."

"Standard procedure," I said.

"Right. The coroner conducted the autopsy that evening and recovered small bits of stone from Sartor's hair and scalp where he apparently bumped his head on a hard surface and fell into the pool. But the bits don't match any substances from the patio or pool area. The patio and pool have smooth surfaces: pressed wooden boards from the back door to the patio, and flagstone tiles—pale yellow, brown, and pinkish—around the pool and cabana. The skirt around the pool is smooth green tile, no chips.

"Our lab tried to match up the bits of stone found in his scalp with the tiles around his pool. No match. We postulate from the abrasion on the side of his head that Sartor slipped when he was entering or exiting the pool, fell in, and drowned. But we can't identify where he fell before he ended up in the pool. His head didn't impact the metal ladder into the pool. We're puzzled about where the stone fragments came from that impacted his scalp and hair."

"Hmm. I see. Something's missing."

"Correct."

"What are the possibilities?"

"We don't know. We've cleared your former wife as a suspect, since she was in Burbank, and we can't identify anyone who would benefit from Sartor's death. But the stone fragments are a puzzle. Until we resolve that issue, it remains an open case —an unfortunate accident. But the stone fragment issue could turn it into a homicide."

The room was silent. The word homicide has a way of making people stop and think of the consequences. I was feeling uneasy. I didn't work in homicide, merely computer security and corporate white-collar crimes.

"Sooo," I said slowly, waiting for one of them to say more, but they remained silent, looking at me. "Again, why are you telling me all this?"

Lamont answered, "When we're stuck in an investigation, we go back over all the testimony and evidence, look at it from all angles, and throw out all sorts of things to reconsider. One of those was to tell you about our investigation and ask for your help."

"What can I do?" I said with a shrug, squirming in the hard, uncomfortable chair.

Lamont pursed his lips again, a facial expression he seemed to use when he wanted to make a point. "One of the things we're considering is that your former wife might know something that she hasn't told us yet. She's just one of the people we want to interview again. Your name came up when we were reviewing her statements to us, and we wanted to see if you would help us.

Your former wife hasn't resisted questioning. She behaves professionally—a confident, very self-assured woman. I don't think she's lying, but we don't have any leads or suspects in the event it wasn't an accident. The stone fragments are a puzzle that keeps us going back over and over all the evidence."

"I understand. But what does this have to do with me?"

Lamont took a deep breath and let it out slowly, like he needed a few more seconds to ask a delicate question.

"Well, Max, we'd like to ask for your help."

"What do you mean?"

The tension was back in the room. I was uncomfortable just being there. Lamont spoke deliberately, pausing between phrases to let his message sink in. "We'd like to know if you'd be willing to reestablish contact with your former wife, purely socially, of course, and hear what she might say about the accident. That is, if she will even talk to you about it at all. The experience was a trauma for her, no doubt. We're just looking for any angle to close the case and confirm that it was an accident."

I didn't know how to respond. I was uncomfortable with their request to reach out to Amanda. I looked left to right, at Freeman, Lamont, and Hopgood, each waiting for my response. I said firmly, "I'm skeptical. I haven't talked to Amanda in more than two years. She'd be suspicious if I called her."

Lamont paused before he made his final request. "Your call, Max. We just want you to think about it and consider helping us."

"All right. I will."

* * *

I talked to Dad after the conference, telling him about the conversation with the LAPD and their request that I get in touch with Amanda. I told him about the details of their investigation, the stone fragments, Amanda's alibi, and my hesitance to get involved, and I asked his advice about meeting them in LA for a full briefing or simply turning them down. I wasn't keen to approach Amanda, particularly about the death of her former boyfriend.

"It's your call, son," Dad said. "Your mother and I will support whatever you decide. You know Amanda better than anyone."

"It's been a long time, Dad. Don't you think she'd be suspicious if I called her out of the blue and asked to get together? If the tables were turned, I'd be surprised if she called me."

"I'm sure you would," he said. "But I can understand why the LAPD contacted you; their investigation has led them up a blind alley. They're probably checking out a number of things to close the case. Amanda has a good alibi; she wasn't there that night or the next morning. Forensics found fragments that don't match any surface from Sartor's patio. That's driving the LAPD nuts: How did the fragments get into his hair? If they knew, they could close the case—accidental death. Move on to the next case."

"I don't know how my talking to Amanda would help," I said. "She might not want to talk about it. It's an embarrassing, unhappy chapter in her life."

"The LAPD is just doing their job, Max. When you're stuck in an investigation, you go over all the evidence, hoping some little piece is hidden under a stone you haven't turned over. You happen to be one of the stones. You were married to Sartor's girlfriend; maybe you can learn something that they can't."

* * *

I called Lamont a week later after sleepless nights and conversations with my supervisor. Like Dad, he said he decision was up to me. In the end, I decided to meet with them again.

I flew down the next week and was picked up at LAX by a police car that drove me downtown to the LAPD. Lamont, Freeman, and Hopgood were waiting in Lamont's corner office with three other officers. The room had been set up with a wide screen against a wall and a projector and stack of folders on a table.

Lamont thanked me for coming and immediately began the meeting. "Our forensic team will show you evidence from the scene, more photos, and aerial views of Sartor's home."

Three hours later, they had finished their presentation, and we were in shirtsleeves around the table, which was strewn with photos, police reports, and plastic evidence bags.

Lamont summarized their investigation and then said, "So, you've heard all that we know, Max. Do you have any questions?"

"No, sir. I understand. It's puzzling for sure."

He sipped his coffee, looked around at his colleagues, and said, "We want to close this case and resolve the dilemma of the stone fragments. We're searching for anything that might help us determine where they came from."

"Yes, I understand."

It was quiet in the room. Someone shuffled their feet under the table. Hopgood cleared his throat.

"Max, we realize we're asking about a sensitive part of your personal life in asking you to contact your former wife and set up a meeting—something social—lunch, dinner, a drink after work —whatever you feel is appropriate," Lamont said. "The form of the meeting is up to you. You understand the dynamics of your relationship and know what would be appropriate. But certainly don't divulge any information we've shared with you. If the first meeting goes well, possibly meet with her again. Without being direct, see if she opens up about the accident."

I contemplated how to approach Amanda after such a long time. If she detected that my motives were to assist the LA police, she'd be furious and refuse to talk. I wouldn't lie to her, but I would withhold my reasons for contacting her. She could politely tell me she didn't want to talk, much less meet. Or she could agree to meet—and then what would happen? No one— not even I—knew the answer to that question.

21

———————

Deb and I had scheduled a long weekend in Portland after my return from Los Angeles. We had talked frequently since the Las Vegas convention, but I hadn't mentioned the LAPD development. It was too delicate to bring up during a long-distance call—too many trip wires. I rationalized it was better to tell Deb in person.

I didn't know how she'd respond to my seeing Amanda again. She could be supportive but cool, jealous, or even livid. In the months that Deb and I had been seeing each other, our college friendship had evolved into a budding romance. Our times together had been fun and uncomplicated, like most new dating situations. We swapped "happy news" about our lives and had no letdowns or silly dramas.

I drove down from Seattle, Deb flew in, and we stayed Friday night at a B&B in Old Town near the Willamette River.

The manager of the B&B recommended we go to McMenamins Crystal Ballroom for dinner. He raved about how popular local brewpubs were, with one opening almost every month in town, which was where craft breweries had first appeared in the 1980s.

Deb and I walked up Burnside and joined a boisterous crowd lined up to go into the hundred-year-old ballroom. It took twenty minutes before a tattooed waitress led us through the noisy crowd to a table near the stage and gave us beer menus. She recommended we order our beers right then, since it was a busy Friday night. We pointed at two recommended beers, and she hurried back toward the bar.

A Celtic rock group was performing onstage, with amplifiers blaring out guitar chords and singers chanting in Gaelic. There was shouting and foot-stomping. A video of the group played overhead on a large screen.

Customers shouted out drink orders to white-aproned college waiters maneuvering through the crowd carrying trays of golden, reddish, yellow, black, and pumpkin-colored pints of foamy beer.

Our waitress was back five minutes later with our pints: Rogue Chocolate Stout for me and Mirror Pond Pale Ale for Deb. We sipped, and Deb gushed, "Yumm. That tastes so good— fresh, hoppy, a real thirst-quencher. I think we'll need another."

"I'm sure we will. I'm thirsty!" I shouted back. We listened to the music, tapping along to the heavy rock beat, the whole ballroom throbbing with the loud music and boisterous crowd.

"I love it here!" Deb shouted as she sipped her beer. "I'm glad the guy at the B&B told us about this place. The band has a real edge, doesn't it? Folksy with a rock beat."

"It sure does, but it's hard to talk," I shouted over the blaring amplifier.

Deb flipped through the menu, reading the list of beers and the history of the ballroom on the back. "This beer menu is pages and pages long! Look at the funky names, Mirror Pond, Hair of the Dog, Hazelnut Brown, Wicked Medicine. There's more than a hundred, and all from Oregon."

"Seattle has great craft beers, too," I said, finally able to talk normally after the band finished a song with a shattering crescendo of guitars, drums, and screaming. "I try a new style every time I go out. Hefeweizen is my newest favorite, fruity with a hint of spice. And cloudy, like fog."

She laughed. "Max, you sound like a beer geek! Beer is for drinking, not writing poetry!"

"Wait until you try one," I said, signaling to the our waitress and ordering two Widmer hefeweizens. We finished our first beers by the time she returned with another tray of clinking pints, frothy foam running down the glasses. She scooped up our empty glasses and set down our new pints before dashing off to serve others.

Deb sipped her pint, and her eyes widened. "Max, you're right. I love this! Great choice—and it is foggy."

It was that kind of evening, talking about beer and planning a fun weekend. It was hard to keep our hands off of each other. It was great to be with Deb; her carefree spirit was infectious.

We strolled arm in arm back to our B&B after three beers, carne asada burritos, two bowls of chips, guacamole, and salsa while sitting through a set with a punk girl band dressed in pink. The girls had pranced across the stage, torturing their guitars and belting out raunchy songs to the cheers of the packed ballroom.

"Boy, wasn't that fun?" Deb said. "Noisy as a locomotive, but what a great place. I haven't drunk so much beer since college. We should come back here in the summer. The Pacific coast is an hour or two away. We could go hiking or mountain biking in the Cascades. Portland has a real verve. Everybody raves about how cool it is here. If I were younger, I'd pick up stakes, move here, start a new life, and hook up with neat people. I'm so glad we came," she said, squeezing my hand. "We're going to have a great weekend! Hey, we better get to our B&B soon! All that beer is flowing through me fast!"

We ran a few steps hand in hand and then slowed to a fast walk, jostling each other along the way and giggling about our fun evening.

It wasn't a good time to tell her about the LAPD and their

request for me to meet Amanda. I wasn't going to spoil our reunion night; Deb was too lively and romantic.

Half an hour later, drunk and giddy, we slipped naked into bed. We cuddled under the covers, beginning an erotic teasing, planting kisses on each other's faces and necks, hands roving over bodies, surrendering to a night of tender passion.

* * *

The next morning, we arose early and drove through the Columbia River Gorge toward snowy Mount Hood. "Thank God we didn't have hangovers this morning, Max. Beers don't give you hangovers unless you put away a gallon. By the way, can we have more beer at lunch? I want to try something new."

"I'll be ready. Let's wait until at least noon. We can walk around afterwards to wear it off."

We had lunch and beers at the Baldwin Saloon in The Dalles and then visited the Fort Dalles Museum. Deb talked the whole time, jabbering about her job, her friends, and how happy she was that we were seeing each other. I shared anecdotes about living in Seattle as I waited for a good time to tell her my news.

We drove up to the north side of Mount Hood, where Deb swooned at the slopes and views all the way to Mount Saint Helens and Mount Rainier to the north.

"We should ski here sometime," Deb said. "I like skiing in Colorado, but I like to try new places. Plus, Colorado doesn't have volcanos. Pretty cool, aren't they? Mount Hood, what's left of Mount Saint Helens, and Rainier."

I decided to wait. Debra was in a joyous mood, talking about planning a summer vacation together. She had been reading travel books about Spain, saying we should go to Madrid and Barcelona in the summer.

"Why don't you start learning Spanish? If we go, we'll want to know how to order meals, find a restroom, and rent a car."

"Great idea. I could sign up for a course at a community college."

"Oh, do it!" she exclaimed, slapping my shoulder. "We'll learn a little español. A high school friend spent a summer in Barcelona and came back with 'wow' stories about backpacking, going to Costa del Sol, and living with a host family who drove her all around the country. I wish I could have done something like that, but I worked summers at a pizza joint before I went to NDSU. I made it into a gig, joking with male customers about eating too much fat and needing to get exercise so they didn't become blimps. Their girlfriends and wives loved it. I made up funny names for them. They kept coming back so I could tease them. The pay was lousy, but I made great tips!"

"You're a character," I said with a smile. "I can just see you, flirting and carrying on. That's Deb."

She changed the subject. "I wonder how you say 'make love' in Spanish," she said with a pixie grin.

"No idea. I never took Spanish. Only two years of German."

"Me neither. But if we go, I want to learn the 'F' word and a few other dirty words—just in case someone uses them."

I couldn't spoil Deb's mood. She was deliriously happy, uninhibited, acting like a teenager. I loved it. My news would be a cold shower. Later.

We returned to Portland, changed clothes, and jumped on the light rail to Waterfront Park. We walked up Burnside to Powell's bookstore, where we browsed for an hour. Deb bought several romance and mystery paperbacks, and I picked up a used copy of Arthur Schlesinger's A Thousand Days. We lugged our purchases in a book bag to dinner at an Italian restaurant in the Pearl District. It was nine thirty by the time we finished our Caesar salad with prosciutto, seafood pasta, and a bottle of Oregon Pinot Noir.

When Deb put down her fork for the last time, she yawned, stretched, and leaned her head on my shoulder. "I'm getting tired. Didn't we have a fun day? Beer at lunch, a bottle of wine with dinner, lots of walking and fresh air. And I've been jabbering like a blue jay all day. You been taking it all in, quiet as a mouse. Tell me to shut up if I talk too much. When I'm with you, I have so many things to tell you. It's like you have a key to my jabberbox."

She giggled. "Jabberbox? That's a new one. Must be the wine." She yawned again, nestling closer. "What's going on in Max's world? Talk to me."

It finally seemed like the best time to tell her; she'd likely go to sleep as soon as we got back to our B& B, and she was flying out the next day. If I waited until then to tell her, she'd be suspicious as to why I waited so long to drop the bomb.

I reached for the wine bottle, poured the last drops into our glasses, and slipped an arm around her shoulder. "There is something I need to tell you."

"Fire away. I'm here but getting drowsy. Don't put me to sleep—nothing boring, please. I might drop off and start snoring." She yawned again, pressing closer.

I took a deep breath and started. "I went to Las Vegas for that tech conference."

"I know. You called me when you were there."

"Three detectives from the LAPD came up to me in the hallway and asked to talk to me in private."

"About what?"

"In a few words, about their investigation into Sartor's death—the Italian director who drowned."

Deb was still for a moment and then raised her head. "Amanda's snarky boyfriend?"

"Yes."

"But why? Is this something about Amanda?"

"Yes," I said, my voice cracking.

"Really?"

She pushed away and stared at me, her eyes shifting from my left eye to my right like she was trying to read my mind. Her hand slid off my arm and onto her lap.

"I don't think I'm going to like this story." She inched farther away, up against the back of the booth.

I held up my hands in defense. "Don't jump to conclusions. Let me tell you the whole story."

So I did, starting with walking out of the panel session and meeting Lamont, Freeman, and Hopgood, who, after introducing themselves, had escorted me to the conference room. When I mentioned they brought up meeting Amanda, Deb held up a hand to cut me off.

"Let's leave. I want to get out of here."

We stood. The waiter came over, Deb excused herself to go to the restroom, and I paid the bill. This wasn't going well.

We left the restaurant separately, Deb opening the door herself and starting down the street ahead of me. I followed, talking faster, wanting to get out the whole story. I quit talking when we got to the B&B. As soon as I unlocked the door to our room, Deb went into the bathroom, took her clothes off, came back in her nightgown, and tossed back the covers on her side the bed.

I hurriedly undressed and went into the bathroom. When I came out, I slipped in on the other side of the bed. I resumed talking about flying to LA and agreeing to their request to meet Amanda.

Deb interrupted me. "I don't want to hear any more. I need to sleep."

I turned out the light, lay back, and closed my eyes. After a minute, I put my arm around her. She lifted it and dropped it like I was contagious with a virus.

In our dark room, the digital clock clicked midnight. The

silence was broken by a siren on the street. A door closed down the hallway. I heard the rustle of clean sheets as Deb shuffled her feet and kicked back some covers. I felt alone and sad.

"Good night, Deb."

"Yeah, 'nite."

I closed my eyes, but sleep eluded me. We were both restless. Deb rolled over a couple of times but then flipped back, keeping her back to me throughout the night.

* * *

A sliver of sunrise coming through the drapes woke me. I rolled over, wanting to doze a few minutes longer. As my brain unfroze, memories of the previous night replayed in my mind. Deb was leaving in a few hours. Could I do damage control and patch up what I'd started?

I rolled over again, rubbed my eyes, and looked around.

Deb was sitting in a chair by my side of the bed, wearing a short white robe, barefoot, legs crossed, arms crossed, staring at me.

I pushed back so I could sit up.

"M-morning," I stammered, wondering how long she'd been awake. "How did you sleep?"

Nothing. Her hair was combed back from her face, and she was staring as if I was something that should be tossed in the garbage.

"Deb?" I tried again. No response.

"Excuse me, bathroom," I said, tossing off the covers and hurrying into the bathroom. I returned with a towel wrapped around me and propped myself up in the bed.

Mute stare. Her crossed leg was pumping furiously.

She finally spoke, her voice cool. "Why did you wait until last night to tell me you were going to see Amanda?"

I held up a hand. "That was a mistake. I'm sorry. But we were having such a good time, and I wanted to wait for the right time to tell you."

"So you wait until our last night, when I'm sleepy and a little drunk, and then you drop this bomb about going to see Amanda. How do you think that makes me feel?"

I sat up. "I wasn't trying to hurt you. I should have told you right away. My fault. Sorry."

"Anything else to tell me? No more bombs, please."

I stressed to Deb that it was Lamont's idea, not mine, that I see Amanda to help the LAPD resolve the stone fragment evidence. I assured Deb that cared about her deeply and had no desire to be with Amanda again.

The more I talked, the more Deb softened. She stopped pumping her leg and propped her chin in her hand, with her elbow on the armrest.

"I want to believe you."

"Please, I want you to. I wouldn't do anything to damage what we have going on."

She raised her eyebrows. "Really?"

I made a crossing movement over my chest. "Cross my heart. I promise." I gazed into her eyes and said, "As I've said before, I love you. I wouldn't do anything to hurt you. Maybe I was too cautious, waiting until last night to tell you."

Deb got up, tucked her robe between her legs, and sat next to me. "Do you really mean that?"

"Absolutely." I put my arm around her and pulled her close.

She resisted, pushing away. "I hope this isn't a surprise, but every woman on the planet has heard stories about a boyfriend reuniting with an old flame, patching things up, and jumping in the sack for old times' sake. The fires are rekindled after wild sex, and the loser ditches his girlfriend. It's a fairy tale both good and bad girls know all about."

"That's not going to happen. Believe me."

"This weekend didn't turn out the way I thought it was going to. I was planning to invite you to Chicago to meet my parents. But I'll hold off on that."

"I understand. We can do that another time."

"It's my dad's birthday. I go every year."

The tension had been broken a bit. At least she was talking and was not as angry as she'd been the previous night. "Want me to make some coffee?" I asked, pointing at the coffee machine.

"Not yet. We're not finished."

"Okay."

"Max, I don't know how to say this, but I have to. You're worth waiting for. Not that I was waiting for you way back in marketing class. I'm not that kind of girl. But never in my wildest dreams did I ever guess that we would be where we are. Don't ask me where that is, because I don't know."

"Portland," I said, hoping to see her crack a smile.

She did. Barely. "Yes, I know that, dummy."

I continued. "Where we are, in that other context, is trying to see if we can be more than a weekend couple."

She blinked. "Oh, yeah? How do you mean?"

"What I think both of us are looking for. A long-term relationship. Not just spending weekends together. It may be a long way off, but one of us would have to move and start a new job."

Deb shook her head. "That's not possible, for a lot of reasons."

"Not now, but sometime, if we start talking about it."

"Are you serious?"

I nodded. "Very serious. I want us to be together."

She sighed, moved closer, and put her head on my shoulder.

"I never thought I would hear you say those words."

"I did. And I meant them."

"Oh, man, oh, man, I gotta put this through the old brain

processor. I've got a file marked 'Boyfriends: good, bad, and all the others.' You're in there someplace. I might have to move you from one file to another. Give me a minute."

"What are you talking about—a file of boyfriends?"

"Oh, I'm kidding. You're saying things I never expected to hear from you. I have to move your card, take it out of an old file, put it in a file with a new name. How about: 'Current boyfriend, long-term relationship—maybe.'"

We both laughed. "That's hilarious. I can picture you doing this. You've never said this before."

"Silly boy. All women have to keep track of the men they've run across in life. I keep a mental file, a list of names in different categories, just in case I run into a guy who acts like someone else I have in an old file."

I roared. "That's so funny! You're terrific. You always keep me laughing."

"I know part of that is a defense. If you make guys laugh, they're less likely to say things that will hurt you."

"Hmm. I never thought of it that way."

"Here's something else to think about, Mr. Big Shot."

"What's that?"

"If we hadn't run into each other at that homecoming a couple of years ago, this wouldn't have happened. Before then, you were just a good-time Charlie I had known in college. But here we are, naked under these robes, having made wild, crazy love the first night, and then having fun driving to Mount Hood, carrying on like crazy teenagers, talking about going to Spain in the summer. It's been crazy fun, but it could be over as fast as you can snap your fingers."

She snapped her fingers to make her point.

"No, it won't be." I grabbed Deb and kissed her, our mouths opening. She stood up and wrapped her arms around my neck. We fell backwards onto the bed, struggling to slip out of our robes.

An hour later, we ordered breakfast delivered to our room. We stayed in bed until noon, threw our clothes on, packed hurriedly, ran down the steps to my car, and raced to the airport. Deb made it to her gate seconds before they closed the aircraft door.

22

Reaching Amanda was a comedy. When I returned home after Portland, I called the last number I had for her.

A young female answered. "Publicity," she said with a dismissive tone.

"I'm trying to reach Amanda Foxx. My name is Max Bauer. I'm her former husband."

"Who?" Her voice came through the phone at high volume.

"Max Bauer, her former husband. This is the only number I have for her."

"Max Bauer, the baseball player?" came her excited answer.

"That's right."

"Really! I'm talking to Max Bauer? My brother lives in Boston. You're his favorite player."

"That's nice. But I'm out of baseball. Have been for a number of years."

"Yeah, that's right. He told me that," she said in a singsong voice, sounding like a giddy teenager. She dragged out the word told like she was in a drama class.

"Is this Amanda's phone number?"

"Uh, no. I work for her publicist. I'm a film student at UCLA. This is a number she had awhile ago. She has another number now."

"Can I have that, please?"

"Sorry, Mr. Bauer, I can't give out her number. We screen calls and pass messages to our clients. You know, a lot of people call—troublemakers, cranks, people who think they can talk to someone just because they've seen their movies."

"Would you like my number?"

"Yes, let me take it down and give it to my boss. She'll call you back when she's off the phone."

Twenty minutes later, a woman called, sounding more mature but hesitant. "Is this Max Bauer?"

"That's right. I want to reach Amanda."

"Sir, we have instructions about giving out client phone numbers. I'll call her and ask if she wants your number."

An hour later, the woman called back. "Sir, I would like to verify that you are who you say you are. Can you answer a question? I'll pass what you say on to Amanda."

"What is this, a game?" I was getting peeved at the runaround.

"To be honest, Mr. Bauer, we get a lot of people who demand our clients' phone numbers. Some are genuine, like I'm sure you are, but there are others who are crackpots or weirdoes. We screen calls and try to verify that the person calling is actually who they say they are."

"What do you want to verify?"

"A simple question: Can you tell me your father's name?"

I told her.

"Thank you. Here's Amanda's phone number." I wrote it down, shaking my head in bewilderment, and called the number. I reached her voice mail.

It felt strange to hear Amanda's voice, even if it was a recording. I could picture her as if she were standing in front of me. The memories were haunting—past events along with the emotions connected to what her voice had once meant to me.

"Hi, it's me," she said in a monotone. "Leave your name and a message. I'll call back when I'm free."

I left a message, trying to sound casual and upbeat. I hung up feeling like I was riding a carousel, going around and around while trying to reach Amanda. I finally got the brass ring when she called twenty minutes later.

"Max, is that you?" Amanda's voice was warm and genuine, not like those in "publicity," whoever they were. "I'm so glad you called! Where are you?"

"Seattle. I've been living here the last several years."

"So nice to hear your voice. It's been a long time. How's my favorite ballplayer—or former ballplayer?" she asked in her familiar, flirtatious style.

"Great. Couldn't be better."

"I've been thinking about you, with spring training under way in Arizona and Florida. I'll bet that's hard on you, with a part of you wishing you were still playing."

"I always feel a little nostalgic this time of year. I can't help it. But that was another life, and I've moved on."

"Good for you. I knew you'd find something after you left the game."

I wanted to get to the point and didn't want to waste time on chitchat. "The reason I'm calling is that I'm going to be in LA next week. I wanted to see if you'd be interesting in having lunch."

"I'd absolutely love to! When are you coming?"

"I'll be there Wednesday. A Seattle friend's parents, who live in LA, are traveling in South America. My friend invited a couple of us to join him and stay at their home for a week. It's been rainy in Seattle all winter. Thought it would be nice to have some sunshine and warm weather."

"This is the place for that. I really love it here. It's been, what, four years since the last time we saw each other? Let's get together."

"If you're free. How's the movie business?"

"Take me to lunch and I'll tell you."

I was glad our call was not long. I just wanted to reach out, connect, and plan to meet.

Amanda chose a French restaurant on Santa Monica Boulevard. I got there early. When she arrived, she looked stunning: tanned, with swept-back short hair that accented her almond eyes and high cheekbones. She was wearing a short teal skirt; a bright, flowery blouse; and heels. Her purse looked like it cost more than I made in a month.

She had changed. She was not the sexy femme fatale from her early movies. She was now more mature, sultry—a beautiful, confident woman. Every male customer and waiter followed her with their eyes as the tuxedoed maître d' led her to my table. We embraced, kissed cheeks, and exchanged gentle pats on the back. The maître d' then pulled back her chair, seated her, and bowed to us. "Enjoy your meal," he said with a French accent.

"You look grrreat, Max," she purred as we separated and took our seats. "I'll bet there's a string of girls a mile long after you. No way I'm introducing you to my girlfriends; they'd snatch you up in a heartbeat." A genuine laugh, no acting.

Amanda knew how to break tension with a little flattery. "Not really," I said, my voice betraying my anxiety. "I have a few women friends, but nothing serious."

"I don't believe you for a minute. You've always had a pretty girl on your arm," she said, hooding her eyes in that sexy way she used in her movies. "You're even more handsome than when you were playing ball. Time's been good to you. I'm at the stage in my life when I find older men sexier than young stallions."

We ordered wine, studied the menu, and made small talk, still a little uncomfortable with our reunion. After we ordered,

Amanda steepled her fingers and looked across at me, a warm smile on her face.

"You really look good, Max, honest. You're aging very well. If I didn't know, I'd guess you were in your twenties."

"I left my twenties a few years ago. I'll be forty before you know it. It's amazing how time flies."

"Isn't that the truth? One day you're in college, wondering what life has in mind for you. You blink, and you have a mortgage, bills, a few aches and pains, and your mirror tells you you're not young anymore."

We both laughed. The soft light created an intimate mood as we sipped our wine. We looked at each other for a couple of moments, neither of us sure how to keep the conversation going.

"You still work out, like when you were playing ball?"

"I run thirty miles a week, play some tennis, and go hiking and mountain biking around Mount Rainier. I'm ten pounds lighter than when I played ball."

"Good for you! Dodgers and Lakers I know turn to jelly doughnuts after they retire. You miss the game?"

"I do," I nodded, relieved that we were chatting casually—little drama, old friends reuniting. "You can walk off the field for the last time, but a part of you still wants to be wearing a uniform and tossing the ball around the diamond."

"I'll bet it does."

"It was a good life, but it's behind me. There's plenty to life after baseball."

"Wonderful attitude. You always were a winner, whatever you did. And what kind of work are you doing now?" She sipped her wine, looking over the rim, more relaxed than I was.

"I work for a small state agency that investigates white-collar crime. Pretty boring, mostly, but I like the analytical stuff—crunching numbers, reading corporate filings, talking to lawyers and accountants."

"Interesting," she said, slightly bored. "You took some computer courses, didn't you?"

"That's right. They helped me get the job." I didn't want to say more, and she didn't ask.

We flirted through the dinner like we had in the old days. It was easy to get back in the groove with Amanda; we had chemistry and both knew it. Old urges were coming back: the desire to reach out and hold hands or to hint at something provocative. I think she felt the same. But we kept the conversation neutral emotionally. We let it flow smoothly, like warm honey, with dashes of self-deprecating humor, funny memories, and updates on our families and people we'd known when we were married.

We spent two hours in the restaurant: two glasses of wine, veal cordon bleu, tiramisu for dessert. When we walked out of the restaurant, we had to shield our eyes from the bright sunlight. I walked her to the parking lot.

Amanda said, "I'm going to a dinner party tomorrow night. Want to be my guest? It's in Malibu—friends I've known for years. No movie people. Old married types, young kids, a real estate agent, a professor at USC. You'd like them. They know about you, of course. I'll just say you're in town for a couple of days."

"Sure. I'd love to."

She gave me the address and said she'd meet me there. It was a pleasant evening with friendly people. Amanda and I sat together. We told stories about living in Boston, and I told a few baseball stories. But Amanda and I kept it light—no hint that we were getting back together, just two friends meeting after a long time. I suspected that Amanda had told her woman friends that they shouldn't read anything into our date; I just happened to be in town for a couple of days.

"That was nice," I said as we left the dinner party and walked toward our cars.

"How much longer are you going to be in town?" she asked.

"I'm going back Sunday night."

"Would you like to go wine tasting on Saturday? There are some wineries north of Santa Barbara. If we get back in time, we can have a quiet dinner. I know a cozy restaurant where we can have privacy."

"Sure, that sounds fine. It would be nice to be outdoors without rain."

She reached up and kissed me on the cheek. "Thanks, Max. I'm glad you called. It's fun seeing you again."

"Same here."

"I'll see you Saturday. Can you drive up to Montecito, where I live?"

"Just give me the directions."

"I'll call tomorrow."

23

I drove to Amanda's home in Montecito, a small town east of Santa Barbara that is home to many celebrities in the entertainment field. It's a quiet area with midsized mansions behind security fences and gates and hillside villas with Mediterranean landscaping.

Through the gates I could see Toyota Land Cruisers, Mercedes-Benz E350s, Lincoln Navigators, and GMC Denalis parked in front of multi-vehicle garages. They all looked shiny, new, and freshly washed.

Amanda's villa was on a hilly cul-de-sac with three elegant homes facing the Pacific Ocean. Five-foot-high walls separated the three homes, all of which were two-story, stucco, Spanish-style houses with red tile roofs. Amanda's was in the middle, with a curved driveway that led to a security gate. I drove up and punched the code she had given me, and the gate swung open.

I drove up a slight grade, spotted a swimming pool to my right, and parked alongside a white limousine in front of a two-car garage. A short Hispanic man wearing a dark suit, white shirt, and red bow tie was standing by the limousine.

When I got out, he raised his sunglasses and said, "Good morning, sir. I'm Roberto. I'll be your driver today."

"Good morning," I said with a nod. I turned around to look at the pool. Very nice. Oval-shaped and long enough to swim laps. A floating pool sweeper whished over the surface, swallowing wind-blown leaves. Four lounge chairs were set around a circular stone table with an umbrella propped in the center. The pool area was partially shaded by tall cycads, banana palms, and tree ferns that reached above the stucco wall separating her home from her neighbors.

The cobalt blue water was shimmering in the morning sunlight, an appealing site for someone who'd spent the winter in chilly, rainy Seattle. I was tempted to take off my shoes and socks, roll up my pants, and put my feet in the cool water. I'm sure it was heated.

Amanda's patio looked like a desert botanical garden. In the area between her home and the pool were dozens of euphorbia, aloe, bromeliads, and barrel cacti set in a bed of smooth river stones in pale gold, bronze, and beige.

"Good morning, Max!" Amanda called out as she walked out of her screened patio. She looked stunning, in tan slacks; a short-sleeved, flowered, blouse; and a yellow sweater over her shoulders. Her hair was tied back in a scarf bun.

She was a Southern California beach girl living very comfortably. And alone.

She wore a welcoming smile as she walked toward me carrying two metal coffee mugs. She offered a cheek for me to kiss.

"Welcome to my home. Isn't it a beautiful day!"

"It sure is. Sunny and warm—not what I'm used to."

She handed me a coffee, looped her arm with mine, and led me toward the limo. "I hired a limo for the day. Roberto will drive so we can taste wine and not worry about driving home."

"Good idea."

"I thought you'd like some coffee. You still take cream, no sugar?"

"That's right."

I took a sip of the hot, steamy coffee. "Thanks."

The morning sun was shining on her face, making her pale green eyes sparkle like jewels.

"Let's get started," she said, moving me toward the limo. Roberto opened the back door and gestured for us to enter his tinted-windowed, sunroofed chariot.

The interior was a mini party room, with plush gray carpeting, rolled leather bench seats, a table with cup holders, a miniature refrigerator, a TV monitor and a sound system. A glass privacy window separated the limo's backseat from the front.

We got in, Roberto closed the door, and we drove out, the gate shutting behind us. Roberto cruised through Montecito's narrow streets toward Highway 1.

"Oh, how rude of me!" Amanda said as we pulled onto Highway 1. "I didn't give you a house tour! I'm sorry. We can do it when we get back."

"You have a beautiful home. How long have you had it?"

"Three years. I got a great price for my bungalow, and my real estate agent kept telling me she had an ideal place that I'd love. And I did! It has four bedrooms, not just two; a larger kitchen; a dining room; and the pool. I love the pool! I heat it in the winter so I can swim almost every day. The neighbors are friendlier, much better than in Hollywood."

I learned that she had sold her home a year after our divorce. Our divorce agreement had said each of us would own our homes separately.

Amanda and I sipped our coffee while she showed me a map of wineries in Happy Canyon, Solvang, Santa Maria, and the Santa Ynez Valley. She had made a reservation for lunch at one of the vineyards in Solvang.

"You're getting the grand tour. Roberto has a list of the

wineries we'll visit and a nice place where we'll have lunch. I've taken friends on my wine tour when they visit me. I even took my mother last summer."

"Really? How did she like it? I can't imagine Olive on a wine tour."

She laughed. "You're right. She liked it but kept asking me how much everything cost, my home, the limo, vacations, even my clothes. She's obsessed about having enough money to retire; that's all she talks about. I tell her I'll help her, but she says she can't take money from me. She has this old fogy Midwestern ethic that you don't go into debt or accept money from people."

"Sounds familiar. My parents are the same way. I bought them a new car when I signed with Boston. Dad sends me a check every year to make annual payments. I just tear it up and tell him it was a gift."

Our conversation flowed easily as we visited wineries in Buellton, Solvang, and the Santa Ynez Valley, tasting Syrahs, Pinot Noirs, Zins, Chardonnays, and Cabernets.

Amanda said she loved working in the movie industry, and she told me about scripts she was reading and her next movie shooting in Montreal.

When she asked about my work, I made it sound unglamorous: doing research, meeting lawyers, helping them draw up legal documents. She smiled politely, nodded, asked few questions.

We had dinner at the Mirabelle Restaurant in Solvang. Amanda invited Roberto to have dinner in the dining room, we were in a cozy back room with a fireplace and a window looking out on the backyard garden, which was lit up with floodlights.

After we ordered and were having our first glass of wine, Amanda rested her elbows on the table and steepled her fingers. "You've been a good listener. I'm happy we had the afternoon to catch up on each other's work and social lives."

"Yes, it has been wonderful. Thanks for planning this."

She reached over and touched my hand. "There's one thing, I haven't brought up. I'm sure you've been wondering if I was going to tell you about that messy scandal awhile back."

Amanda's eyes signaled she was looking for permission to tell me. The wine had lubricated our conversations. We were talking like old friends, sharing good things in our lives, complimenting each other often, almost reaching intimate matters.

I shrugged, trying to appear nonchalant. "It's a private matter. We've had a pleasant day with no agenda, just sharing memories and what our lives are like."

She nodded, going on. "It has been nice, but in the interest of full disclosure, I think I should tell you."

"It's up to you."

She sipped her Pinot Noir, set the glass down, and then splayed her hands in front of her as if it was a businesslike matter.

"I want to. You were the closest person to me for many years. I don't have anything to hide from you."

I leaned back in my chair, giving her all my attention.

"First of all, the media did a miserable job exploiting me and saying hurtful things. My publicist said I should ignore them and not get in a catfight with them, because they always win. I went into seclusion and stayed away from the social scene for a couple of months. I'm so thankful that my friends stuck with me through that dreadful time."

The waiter brought our dinner. We started eating, remaining quiet for a couple of minutes. If Amanda wanted to continue, it was going to be at her initiative. I wasn't going to ask questions. I wanted to let her tell her story her way.

"Well, a little backstory. I first learned about Damiano when I took a course in foreign cinema at NDSU. We watched French, Japanese, Australian, and Italian films and had to write a paper for our final grade. I chose Italian films, and when I was doing research, I read an interview with Damiano, who had apprenticed with a famous director, Zeno Moresdo. Damiano was very handsome and had a beautiful wife and two young kids. When he was only twenty-nine, he made his second film, *Casanova's Homecoming*, which won a bunch of international awards. I saw it in Cambridge when you were on a road trip. I told you about it when you came back."

"Hmm, I don't remember. You mentioned a lot of movies. Doesn't ring a bell."

"No matter. A few years later, when I was working in films, I heard he was living half the year in Los Angeles, promoting his vision to have Italian actors appearing in American movies and American actors in Italian movies.

"I met him at a party and told him I had written a paper about him in college. He invited me to lunch. He was very charming. We went out a few times, and he invited me to fly to Italy and come on the set of a movie he was making. Not my style—soft porn, which makes money but gets panned by critics. Afterwards, he wanted me to meet his family in the Veneto area, in a village called Bassano del Grappa. We went. I met his mother, his sister and her family from Milan, and his teenage sons, who live with their mother in Padua.

"The week was like a fairy tale—this wonderful family, his sister's children running around, his mother fixing amazing pasta dishes, all of us sitting in the kitchen drinking wine, singing Italian songs, his friends stopping by for dinner. In the evenings, we went for walks around his village and into the vineyards. It was magical. That's the only word that describes it."

She sipped her wine, dabbed her lips with a napkin, and continued.

"The next week, Damiano took me to Venice, my favorite Italian city. We took a gondola ride through the canals, had a moonlight dinner at Murano, walked through St. Mark's piazza, and climbed to the top of the campanile for incredible views of the lagoons."

"Sounds interesting. I've never been to Venice."

"Then, when we got back to California, he talked about getting married. I was flattered, but I really wasn't ready. He said he'd wait. When we first started dating, he swore he'd be faithful to me. And he was. But after we returned from Italy, I started being suspicious. His stories became more elaborate about what he was doing when we were apart. I had heard stories about him with other women, and we had an argument in a restaurant. I walked out when I caught him in a lie."

Her hand was shaking when she picked up her wine. Her face was pale, drawn, like someone had pumped the life out of her.

She checked her watch. "It's getting late, Max. We won't be home until ten thirty. Do you want to spend the night? It's too late to drive all the way back to Santa Monica."

"Well, I don't know," I said, surprised by her invitation. Why would she want me to spend the night at her house?

She punched me lightly on the arm. "Don't worry, Max. I have a guest room where you can sleep. We can go for a swim in the morning before you leave."

24

Saturday night traffic on Highway 1 through Santa Barbara was clogged with folks leaving bars and restaurants along State Street to drive back to LA or homes along the coast. We didn't arrive at Amanda's until eleven thirty, sleepy from a long day of sampling wines followed by dinner in Solvang.

After Roberto drove away, Amanda led me inside her home and gave me a brief tour of the downstairs, the new kitchen, the dining room, the studio where she worked, and the four bedrooms upstairs. She took me to one of the guest rooms, checked the bathroom for fresh towels, and told me there were extra swimsuits in the closet. She kissed me on the cheek.

"I'm glad you'll stay over. We'll have breakfast in the morning and go for a swim. Then you can be on your way."

"Good idea. A swim sounds nice. Thanks for your hospitality."

We hugged briefly and then she stepped back, our fingers still touching. "It's been great seeing you, Max. Thanks for coming."

No funny business, no sly attempt at seduction, no clinches. I was relieved.

I didn't wake up until seven thirty, when I heard her splashing in the pool. I took a quick shower; put on one of the swimsuits, a robe, and slippers; and went downstairs to the patio. The bright morning sun rising over the San Gabriel mountains shimmered on the fronds of palm trees that gently waved in breezes coming off the Pacific.

Amanda was swimming laps in a yellow bikini, wearing goggles, her robe draped over a lounge chair. I sat down and watched until she finished. She climbed the tile steps at the shallow end and emerged, water dripping off her elbows and chin, a smile glowing on her face. "Jump in and take a dip! Water's warm. You'll love it!"

I took off the robe, got up on the diving board, and dove in, bracing for the shock of cool water. But the water was warm and soothing, and when I surfaced, I let out a whoop and continued swimming to the end, looking over to see Amanda toweling off and roping a towel turban over her wet hair. I swam another lap and saw her put on a robe and go inside. I continued swimming, my muscles stretching with each stroke, making me feel alert and fully alive on that bright California morning. I loved her place.

When I finished my laps, Amanda came out carrying a tray with steaming coffee mugs, plates of toast and bagels, a bowl of strawberries, bananas, and a pitcher of orange juice.

"Feels great, doesn't it?" she said as I toweled off and put the robe back on. "I love morning swims. It gets my day off to a good start."

We sipped coffee, nibbled the toast and bagels, ate the fruit, and recalled our wine tasting adventure. The sun was warming the air by the minute. In half an hour, it would be hot enough for another dip before I left.

"Yesterday was wonderful. That's the best time I've had in years."

"Same for me."

"You've always been fun. I miss our good times." She raised her orange juice. "A toast to us, a nice reunion. Let's do this again sometime." We clinked. A red flag: It was the first hint that she was interested in rekindling our relationship.

She lowered her sunglasses. "Question."

"Sure, fire away."

"No girlfriends? I find that a little hard to believe."

I shrugged. "I'm not in a rush. The right girl hasn't come along."

She ran a finger around her juice glass. "That doesn't sound like you. What's holding you back?"

I shrugged. "Well, I've been involved with a couple of very nice women, but nothing lasted more than a year."

"There's no honey back in Seattle waiting for you?"

"Nope." Truth. Debra didn't live in Seattle. "I saw Deb recently in Portland."

"Deb who?"

"From NDSU. She introduced us, remember?"

"Oh, that Deb. Of course I remember. How is she?"

"Great. She has a good job and travels a lot with Procter & Gamble."

"That's nice. Tell her hi for me. She was funny. A golf jock. Hung out with all the athletes."

I held my breath, not wanting this conversation to go on. I sipped my orange juice, reached for another strawberry, and popped it in my mouth. Time to turn the tables.

"How about you? You haven't mentioned anyone you're involved with."

She shook her head. "Nope. I haven't slept with anyone in months. I've missed having sex with you. It would have been nice to sleep together last night, but you're cautious. And I can wait."

Time to throw another block. "But I'm sure you're surrounded by attractive, eligible men all the time."

"Oh, don't worry about that. It's just publicity," she said, waving a hand like she was swatting a fly. "Publicists set up those things. Those men don't mean a thing. They're props. If they're not gay, they're cheating on their wives, looking for a shack job, or trying to screw their way into my next movie."

"Oh."

"I've been out of the limelight for several months. I don't miss it." She wrinkled her brow like she was remembering something that she didn't want to talk about.

We had reached an impasse. Time to sip coffee, nibble a bagel, peel a banana. A few moments of silence passed while we both tried to figure out how to break the silence.

Amanda spoke first. "Max," she started, slowly drawing out my name. "Are you resisting me?"

She was persisting, inching me to a cliff I wanted to avoid. "We've had a nice few days. You've been very hospitable. But I fly home tonight, and tomorrow we resume our lives in different cities. Life goes on."

She nodded, maintaining her poise, not ready to concede. "I know what's holding you back. It's that thing about Damiano."

My blood pressure was rising; we were approaching perilous waters. What else did she want to say?

"It took a lot of courage to tell me about him last night."

She nodded and looked away. "Yes it did. It is difficult to talk about it. But I trust you."

She looked past me toward the Pacific, her eyes masked behind her sunglasses. Her chest rose and fell as she clutched her robe to her neck like she was chilled. But the morning was becoming warmer, the sun higher and brighter. It was going to be a gorgeous day.

I had a flash memory of the night Amanda and I met, when I had felt strong sexual attraction to her. Now, once again, my senses were more acute, just as they had been that first night at the bonfire. I smelled the dank, salty breeze and heard the cry of seagulls swooping overhead, the rustle of palm leaves in the garden, and the gurgle of the pool cleaner slurping across the water.

I could almost hear the gears working in her brain, calculating what she would say next.

"Do you want to know more? Everything?"

I felt a jolt of electric tension in the air, as if a bolt of lightning was about to crack. Amanda was escalating a painful memory from her past in some kind of exorcism.

"I'm not pressuring you."

"But it will always be there. We can't move forward until I come clean about my past."

"Your call."

"Okay. Give me a few minutes."

She got up, went into her house, and was gone for about ten minutes. I was puzzled by Amanda's persistence in bringing up her affair with Damiano, but I figured she might be feeling guilty about something, and talking about it with someone she had once been close to might help her live with that.

I opened my robe to feel the warm sun on my chest, knowing I'd be back in chilly Seattle in a few hours. Ocean breezes fluttered the palm trees, ferns, and cycads. The temperature seemed to be rising every minute.

Amanda had a great life: a beautiful home, a good career, a busy social life, all anyone could hope for. But I sensed something was missing in her life. She needed someone to love, to spend lazy, sunbaked Sunday mornings with swimming laps, planning a relaxing day.

Amanda slid open the glass door. She was carrying a tray with a glass pitcher of Bloody Marys, a crystal bowl of ice cubes, glasses, a plate with celery and lime wedges, and a bottle of tabasco sauce.

She set the tray on the table and stirred the Bloody Mary pitcher with a glass spoon as if it were a chemical brew. Beads of moisture trickled down the chilled pitcher.

"You like Bloody Marys?"

"I sure do."

She filled two glasses, dropped in ice cubes, stuck in a celery stalk, added a dash of tabasco, and slipped lime wedges onto the rim.

She handed a glass to me and picked up her own.

She reached over to clink my glass. "A toast, to a reunion, and maybe a new beginning." Her tone was touching, almost a pleading.

We sipped, eyes locked over the rims of the glasses. I set mine back on the table. Amanda leaned back and lowered her sunglasses. "I have a confession, Max."

"Confession?"

"I didn't tell the police everything." It came out in a whisper, like a child confessing about a stolen cookie.

I sucked in my breath, reached for my glass, and took another drink. She crossed her legs, her robe falling open to her bikinied stomach.

"Mmmm. I love Bloody Marys in the morning. I don't do this often, but it's a special occasion. You're leaving today. We'll have a little celebration—a few nice days together."

I nodded, figuring that she was stalling before continuing with what she called a confession.

She looked at me pensively, as if she was trying to anticipate how I would react to what she was going to say.

"What I didn't tell the police was that I didn't spend the night at the cottage."

I raised my eyebrows. "Oh?"

"I went to a restaurant with a friend I'm mentoring, Pauline

Cox. I've done her favors, introduced her around, even got her a small role in a movie. I asked if she would return a favor."

Where was she going with this?

Amanda took a long drink and lowered her glass to her lap, her eyes on the pool cleaner slurping along the surface. "I knew Damiano was having a party that night. A little bird told me that afternoon. It was his regular party gang, including an Italian bimbo he'd been drooling over. He always had his eye out for an easy mark; she was his latest. Damiano had a reputation for bedding starlets between his two wives and assorted girlfriends. I'd heard stories about him, of course, but he told me he would be faithful to me.

"I spent the day on the set in Burbank, went to dinner with Pauline, and asked if she would drive my car to my cottage and spend the night. We exchanged sweaters and hats in the parking lot, and I drove her car to her apartment and spent the night there. I knew security cameras in the lot would see my car drive in. But at night, wearing my hat and sweater, she could pass for me. Same height, hair color, figure. We almost look like sisters."

Another sip, eyes staring at the pool. "I got up at 5:00 a.m., drove to Damiano's home, parked a block away, and walked through the alley. I was going to confront him when he came out for his morning dip. I wanted to embarrass him and tell him it was over and I never wanted to see him again."

I held my breath. "I see."

"It was a still dark when I got there; no moon. I walked into his neighbor's yard. There are bushes between their houses. The neighbor was putting in a new patio, and there were stacks of bricks, shovels, and sand in the driveway.

"At dawn, lights come on in Damiano's bedroom and bathroom. He's an early riser. I saw the bimbo take a shower, dress, and kiss him before she drove away."

I took another drink. My heart was racing as she told her

story. Amanda reached for the pitcher and refilled her glass. Her third Bloody Mary? I hadn't started my second.

"A few minutes later, Damiano came out in his robe, stretched, and dipped his toe in the water. He took off his robe, draped it over a chair, went to the diving board, dove in, and swam a few laps."

She took a sip. And another. "I picked a brick off the pile and crawled through the bushes. He climbed the ladder, went over to a chair, and sat down. He likes the morning sun. I crept up behind, ready to confront him, tell him I knew about his party, the bimbo, and that I never wanted to see him again. But standing behind him, watching him comb through his hair with his fingers, I just lost it."

She raised the glass to her lips, took another drink, and dabbed her lips with the edge of her robe.

"This is so hard, but I want to tell you. I think I'm doing the right thing, telling you?"

I nodded, stone-faced, my Bloody Mary resting on my lap. It was agony hearing her story.

"I raised the brick, and without saying anything, hit him on the side of the head. It stunned him. He grabbed his head, leaned out of the chair, and fell forward into the pool. He struggled a few seconds, then stopped, facedown. It only took a few seconds. I was paralyzed, couldn't speak, shaking all over. He was floating, arms out, moving with the water. It was so quiet. It all happened so fast. What could I do? He drowned in seconds."

I could picture the scene. I felt shocked that Amanda's rage had made her commit a violent, murderous act.

Amanda took another sip of her drink and continued.

"I was shocked, couldn't believe what I had done. I went there to argue with him, tell him it was over, but seeing his bimbo naked in the bedroom, and Damiano looking so virile and confident when he came out to the pool, something triggered in my brain, and I lost control."

Tears flooded her eyes. She shook her head. Waves of grief washed over her. I reached over and put my hand on her arm. She kept crying, her chest rising and falling, her head dropped forward.

She lifted her head and brushed her nose against the sleeve of her robe. "I replaced the brick on the pile, ran to my car, and left. I was crying all the way back to my cottage shocked at what I'd done. I pulled over once, bawling like a baby. When I finally made it back to the lot, I wore sunglasses, lowered my hat, parked at my cottage, went in, and told Pauline what I'd done. She promised she'd keep it a secret, and she has."

Amanda wiped her eyes, leaned back, and let out a sigh, avoiding looking at me. Another sigh, and she turned to me.

"I'm sorry you have to hear this, but I felt I had to tell you. I think . . . it was the best thing I could do."

From the pool, we heard a car pull up in her driveway and stop at the iron gate. We both looked over. I recognized it as an unmarked police car. Three doors opened. Lamont, Freeman, and Hopgood got out and walked to the security gate. Lamont spoke into the intercom.

"Ms. Foxx, I am Detective Lamont, LAPD. Could you please open your gate and let us in?"

Amanda's head snapped back at me, eyes flared open. "Max!" she shrieked. "What is this? Why are the police here? I tell you this terrible thing and the police are at my door? Do you know about this?"

I reached for her hand. "Open the gate, Amanda. Let them in."

She recoiled, lurching back in her lounge chair and tipping over her drink, which shattered, sending glass shards and ice cubes skidding toward the pool.

Tears streamed down her cheeks, her body trembling. Her head jerked back and forth as she looked at Lamont, back at me, and at Lamont again. She started to stand but fell back into the chair.

"Max! Tell me what's happening! Why are the police here?"

I stood up, put one hand on her shoulder and the other hand in the pocket of my robe, where I had put the surveillance mic before going out to the pool. I looked down at Amanda's bewildered stare. Tears were running down her trembling cheeks, her eyes red.

"It's a long story, Amanda. They asked me, I thought you were innocent. I wanted to clear your name. I was doing it for you."

25

———

"**H**ey, come sit down next to me," Deb said. "I've got something for you."

I shuffled over to the couch, my thighs stiff from two days of skiing. I'd always been light on my feet but had shown little of that while negotiating around moguls, racing down double-diamond runs, hitting an ice patch, and tumbling end over end into a snow fence that kept me from colliding into pine trees.

"Little baby have a hard day?" she said, handing me a slim package in silver wrapping paper with a blue bow. "Happy New Year, hot stuff. Or maybe I should start calling you Crash. That was quite a performance on the slopes today. I'm glad I was behind you to get you back on your skis. Pretty wobbly for a while. Ready to go again tomorrow?"

"Naw, think I'll stay by the fireplace, nurse my wounds, and watch the bowl games."

"How about your ego? Did that take a beating as well?"

"It sure did. Give me a couple more years. I might get as good as you."

"You're stalling. Open your present."

I untied the bow, slipped a thumb under the wrapping paper, and opened the box. Inside were my rookie baseball card and a DVD with a cover photo of me in a Red Sox uniform. "What's this?"

"Check it out," she said, pouring us champagne. "It's almost midnight. It's your first gift of the New Year."

"Hey, this is cool. Thanks."

"Let's watch it," she said, snatching it out of my hand and slipping it in the DVD machine. She clicked the remote, and seconds later, the title rolled: Max Bauer Career Highlights: NDSU, Boston Red Sox, Seattle Mariners.

After the title, the opening credits rolled. It was produced by Debra, and the list of "associate producers" included a few team-mates, ESPN, the NDSU coach, and Billy Pampas.

As the opening credits ended, there was the soundtrack of a roaring crowd, probably dubbed from a major league game, and two plays from our CWS series: me hitting a double and sliding under a tag at second base, and me on defense, snatching a line drive inches off the ground and flipping to first base in time to catch a base runner who thought it was going to be a hit.

"This is amazing. I haven't seen this in years. How did you get it?"

"Shush, you at Fenway coming up."

We watched several minutes of TV highlights from when I was playing for the Red Sox, getting hits, scooping up ground balls, and sliding into home plate under a catcher's tag.

Deb cheered when I hit my first home run.

"Way to go, Max! Hit it a mile!"

And then my most cherished memory in baseball.

It was a blistering-hot August afternoon game at Comiskey Park. It was the ninth inning, no outs, and we were ahead by one run. There were two strikes, and the runners on first and second ran on the pitch. The batter cracked a hard liner straight at me, and I caught it. The runner from first was almost on top of me. I tagged him easily and then ran to second myself and dove, tagging the other runner on the foot as he tried to slide back into second. It was the only unassisted triple play of my career, and all the sweeter for being the only one that year in the major leagues.

"Look at that—Gold Glove on defense!" Deb yelled.

I was proud of the memories and thrilled that Debra had pulled them together. When the closing credits rolled, I hugged Deb, nestled next to me, feet tucked under her. There was a blazing fire in the fireplace, and the champagne bottle was half empty.

"That was great! Thanks. A real trip down memory lane."

"I thought you'd like it. Happy New Year, Crash. You were great—my favorite ball player of all time," she said, planting a wet kiss on my sunburned cheek.

I took out a small box from my robe. "Here, a little something for New Year's."

She opened it and took out an engagement ring. "Max! A ring!"

"Deb, will you marry me?"

"Well, of course!" she screamed without hesitation.

The sound of loud booms exploded outside the chalet. Through frost-tinted windows, fireworks ignited the black sky, exploding in brilliant yellow, red, green, and orange rainbows that floated down, sparkling on the slopes and snow-covered trees.

"Happy New Year, honey," I said proudly.

She wrapped her arms around my neck and squeezed, squealing like a puppy.

"I love it! It's gorgeous! Can I put it on?"

"Of course. It's yours."

She plucked it out, slipped it on her finger, held up her hand, and flipped it front and back. The diamonds sparkled in the firelight.

We stayed up another hour, standing by the picture window, watching skiers carrying torches while shushing down snowy slopes in long, snakelike formations—a New Year's Eve tradition.

"Our first New Year's," Deb said, leaning against me. "I don't want to spoil anything, but have you thought about what Amanda's doing tonight?"

I nodded. "Yes, I have. I imagine she's secluded in her Montecito home, where she's been the last few months. Her mom might be there, but they're not close. Maybe she invited over a couple of friends. It'll be a quiet night. Not much to celebrate. Her trial starts in February. Her lawyers have been filing motions for a change of venue and motions for delay, and trying to negotiate down to second-degree murder, even manslaughter."

"You feel sorry for her?"

"I do. But she killed someone. She never should have put herself in that kind of situation. Her motive will be debated at the trial. I'm not a lawyer, but I'm sure she'll end up going to jail."

We were quiet for a couple of minutes, enjoying our wintry holiday but aware that the person who had introduced us, my former wife and Deb's college friend, would be going to prison.

Deb sighed. "It was a career killer, no doubt. I feel sorry for her too. How many people have ruined their lives and the lives of others by making a rash decision when they're under stress. Such a tragedy. She should have waited a day or so after the party, thought through what she was going to say, and dumped the guy after she'd cooled down—telling him he was a cheating creep, a real lowlife. Then she could have left, holding her head up high."

"Yup, you're right. Too bad you weren't there to give her advice."

After the torchlight skiing was over, we sat at the kitchen counter, sipping hot chocolate, reminiscing about our summer vacation in Spain, and discussing our plans for the coming year.

"We're going to have fabulous New Year's celebrations ahead of us. Won't they be fun? Let's plan something special each year."

"Good idea. I'll leave you in charge."

"We'll be married next New Year's. You sure you want to go through with it?" she teased.

"I asked you, didn't I?"

She grinned like a child opening a first Christmas present. "I heard it with my own ears. Best question anyone ever asked me."

We sipped some more champagne. I got up to turn out the kitchen light, which left the living room fireplace casting the only light.

"Quite a year, Max. Last New Year's Eve, I was with girl-friends in Florida. Kinda boring, actually. This New Year's, I'm celebrating with my former marketing classmate, my favorite Red Sox player, and now my fiancé."

"It's been a good year."

"Next year's going to be even better."

"It sure is. Big changes, moving to Boston, living in your Wellesley home."

"And you starting your MBA at Harvard."

"Whoo, whoo! Me at Harvard!" she whooped, flinging the red ribbon from the engagement ring box around her head.

"Can you believe Harvard accepted me? They must have been impressed by my brilliant career as a pizza joint waitress and an NDSU golf jock."

"Hey, you kept moving up, regional manager at P&G."

"I'm going to love living in Boston—"

"Wellesley," I corrected.

"Sorry. I love your home."

"Our home."

"Oops, right. Our home."

"We move in first of March."

"I can't wait. And you starting your new job with the FBI. Think you'll make it to director?"

"Naw, no interest, I just want to work a couple of years and train new agents in Boston. Then we'll follow your career. Think it will be with P&G?"

She shrugged. "Maybe, if they offer me the moon. But Harvard attracts the best corporate recruiters. I'll see what they're offering and decide later. Maybe I'll get off the corporate ladder for a couple years, you know, and get on the mommy track."

"I like that idea. You'll be a great mom."

She winked. "Wanna practice tonight? I'm ready."

THE END

ACKNOWLEDGEMENTS

I would like to thank those who helped me along the way to writing ***Bloody Mary Confession***.

Pamela McManus, my long term and conscientious editor, once again crafted my words into readable prose.

Don Eicher, Lois Scheele, Michele Vannote, Ben Pratt, and David Mumford provided research support. Mike Bruno at the Monterey Police Department offered suggestions on technical issues.

* * *

Thank you for reading ***Bloody Mary Confession***. I hope you enjoyed it and will write a review. Reviews are important for both readers and authors; readers trust other readers and authors value the feedback.

On the site where you read this novel, scroll down past the book details, 'also boughts' and ads. You'll find a link "Write a review." Just click on the link and write a few sentences about what you liked about the book, the plot, characters, dialogue, or suspense.

That's it, easy to do. Thanks!

THE MILAN THRILLER SERIES

I'm currently writing the Milan Thriller Series which features Italy's antiterrorism police, DIGOS (*Divisione Investigazioni Generali e Operazioni Speciali*), at Milan's Questura (police headquarters).

The Milan Thriller Series

Thirteen Days in Milan

Sylvia de Matteo, an American single mother, is taken hostage by terrorists during a political assassination at Stazione Centrale, Milan's train station. She is seized at gunpoint and thrown into the back of a van. Moments later, a Paris-bound train with Sylvia's fiancé and ten-year old daughter aboard departs Centrale without Sylvia. The terrorists drive Sylvia to a warehouse where she is imprisoned in a cell. When the terrorists discover Sylvia's father is a wealthy Wall Street investment banker, they demand a ransom for her safe release.

No One Sleeps

Milan's elite antiterrorism DIGOS police receive a tip that a
sleeper cell of Muslim terrorists have received toxic chemicals
from Pakistan to make deadly sarin gas.
The terrorist leader has access to Milan's centers of finance, technology, commerce, and entertainment--all high profile targets
with potentially hundreds of casualties in a terrorist attack.

Vesuvius Nights

Antonella Amoruso, senior deputy of Milan's antiterrorism
police, receives a call to return to her hometown of Naples for
the funeral of a family member murdered in a Camorra clan feud.
Amoruso is plunged into the dangerous culture of Camorra,
Naple's violent criminal syndicate which thrives on illegal drugs,
prostitution, extortion, and murder. Her goal is to rescue her
family from Camorra's deadly grip.

The Lonely Assassin

A Russian banker embezzles millions laundering money in
Switzerland for Russian oligarchs. He flees with his Italian wife
to a remote location on Lake Como near Milan, where their
daughter lives.

Putin wants him dead and sends a GRU assassin to Milan to
find and poison the banker.

But Milan's antiterrorism police cannot locate the assassin,
Vasily Egorov, who is traveling with phony documents, carrying
a vial of Novichok poison, and speaking Italian. Unexpectedly,
Egorov meets an intriguing Italian woman who probes into his
emotional life. On a dangerous assignment, Egorov realizes he's
an assassin in a deep personal crisis.

What readers are saying about the Milan Thriller Series

"I'm Italian and I must say that Erickson's view of my country and my fellow citizens is not so stereotypical as it appears in other books about Italy written by a foreign writer. His understanding of our political and cultural situation in ***Thirteen Days in Milan*** is very deep, his knowledge about food and drinks amazing, and the characters in the story are powerful and realistic."

"The historical introduction to Italian politics in ***Thirteen Days in Milan*** is very interesting and give a great foundation for the rest of the book. Once you get to know the characters and the story is headed for a big climax it's hard to stop reading. It was easy to visualize the scenes because of the attention to detail in descriptions of the environments, sounds and smells. If you enjoy John le Carre or Raymond Chandler you might enjoy this book."

* * *

"***No One Sleeps*** is a chilling story that reads like today's headlines. With no leads, DIGOS agents use technology to discover that a cell of Muslim terrorists are using stolen phones to communicate. But the agents don't know that the leader of the terrorists is an Italian with Pakistani heritage who was trained at a Taliban terrorist camp in Afghanistan."

"***No One Sleeps*** is a thoroughly researched and soberly told tale of one of today's most pressing issues." KIRKUS REVIEWS

"***No One Sleeps*** is both entertaining and all too real. It is obvious that the author did a great deal of research and although it is fiction, many details are quite accurate, including the training camp in Pakistan. The book is action packed and would make a great movie. It has good plot and character development. I could not put it down."

* * *

"***Vesuvius Nights*** has everything I want in a mystery. A compelling plot, vivid writing, and an Italian setting with vivid details. Erickson's writing style really holds my attention and fully engages me. The pace of the writing mirrors the speed of modern life with the action transpiring over one week. The characters exhibit depth and humanity and become very real. Highly recommended."

"This third book (***Vesuvius Nights***)in Jack Erickson's thriller series moves to Naples with the back story of the leading female detective, exploring the workings of the Camorra, organized crime. Jack's descriptions of Naples and the views of Vesuvius make you feel a part of the vibrant city, and the action will have you transfixed. Can't wait for the next one!"

* * *

"In ***The Lonely Assassin*** Erickson skillfully describes how Putin deals with people who wrong him, even when they leave Russia. I particularly enjoy Erickson's description of the good life in Northern Italy. He also did a very good job of humanizing the 'lonely assassin.' I can't wait for the next book in this series.

"***The Lonely Assassin***" is a cleverly written thriller. The story begins in a bank in Bern, Switzerland. Three Russian government employees are laundering money for Russian oligarch billionaires. One of the three, Dimitri is thought to be off for a few days when another notices that there are some irregular transactions in the accounts Dimitri handles. It quickly becomes apparent that Dimitri has embezzled a substantial amount and he is not just gone for a few days, he is just gone. The news of this crime reaches all the way up to Vladimir Putin who dispatches an assassin to eliminate Dimitri and if necessary his family.

* * *

Thirteen Days in Milan, No One Sleeps, Vesuvius Nights, and ***The Lonely Assassin*** are available as ebooks as well as paperbacks at digital sites or at www.RedBrickPress.net. Your local bookstore can order paperbacks from my Ingram distributor, which does print-on-demand (POD). You'll receive your copy in a couple days.

Book Five in the Milan Thriller Series, ***A Dangerous Friend***, will be published in 2025. You'll receive information about the forthcoming book if you sign up for his newsletter.

www.RedBrickPress.net

www.JackErickson.com

Follow Erickson's international travel at A Year and a Day.

ALSO BY JACK ERICKSON

Milan Thriller Series
Thirteen Days in Milan
No One Sleeps
Vesuvius Nights
The Lonely Assassin

Novels
Bloody Mary Confession
Rex Royale
A Streak Across the Sky
Mornings Without Zoe

Short Mysteries
Perfect Crime
Missing Persons
Teammates
The Stalker
Weekend Guest

True Crime

Blood and Money in the Hunt Country

Noir Series
Bad News is Back in Town

Political Satire
The Next President of the United States

Audio Books
Perfect Crime
The Stalker
A Streak Across the Sky

Nonfiction
Star Spangled Beer:
A Guide to America's New Microbreweries and Brewpubs
Great Cooking with Beer
Brewery Adventures in the Wild West
California Brewin'
Brewery Adventures in the Big East

CHAPTER TWO - THE LONELY ASSASSIN

As a preview of the Milan Thriller Series, here is the second chapter of Book 4, *The Lonely Assassin,* where we meet Dima, the Russian banker in Bern, Switzerland, and his Italian wife, Valeria. They are having their last dinner in Bern at their favorite Italian restaurant. Tomorrow they leave Bern to move to a secret location near Lake Como to be near their daughter who lives in Milan.

Dima knows his life is in danger. Putin will send an assassin after him because he embezzled from Russian oligarchs who were laundering money.

Meet Dima and Valeria . . . .

"I want to make a toast, *amore*," Valeria said, raising a flute of Franciacorta Brut Rosé to her husband at their favorite Italian restaurant in Bern. They were seated at a table on an enclosed outdoor patio looking down on the Aare River and the Kornhausebrucke bridge lit by street lamps.

Sunday dinner at the restaurant was quiet, not like Fridays and Saturdays when Swiss, German, Austrians, Italians and

British and American tourists reserved every table from 7 - 11 PM.

Only two tables were occupied on the patio, beside a stone fountain decorated with pots of flowers. The atmosphere inside the restaurant was decorated with subdued Italian red and white checked table clothes, Renaissance art on the walls, da Vinci, Giotto ceiling in Padua, a Raphael fresco. In the corner, a woman pianist playing arias from Italian operas by Rossini, Bellini, Puccini and Verdi.

"Another toast?" Dima Volkov said, smiling at his wife, her dark eyes sparkling in the twin candles on their table. "We already toasted with champagne at our apartment."

"Yes, *amore*, but that toast was to our last night in Berne. I want to propose another."

"My wife," he said with a grin, "always full of surprises. Let me guess, could it be to our last dinner in Bern?"

"Not really," she said with a smile, raising her glass between the candles. "This one is from my heart."

"From your heart, I like that," he winked.

They clinked glasses, Valeria said in a soft voice, "To my loving Dima who has given me most — " she winked — "of what I wanted in life, a happy marriage, our beautiful daughter, and following me to live in Europe."

She touched her lips, flicked an air kiss. "And most of all, he has given us a new home in Italia!" They clinked, a glow on Dima's face from toasting earlier at home before walking to the restaurant.

"My turn," he said, clearing his throat. Following her example, he held his wine glass between the candles,"To my beautiful, loving, and patient wife."

Valeria laughed, a soft rumble from her throat. She furrowed her brow in a mock gesture of objection. "Patient — me? You have to be kidding! My dear Dima, I'm never patient when I know what I want. Like this beautiful necklace, a nice surprise on our last night in Switzerland."

She placed her palm over a jade necklace he had given her when they toasted at home. "Your persistence is admirable, many women shrink from being clear about what they want. Not me! You're the reason I'm persistent. I know what will make you happy too, like our new home so we can live closer to Chiara."

"She'll be our first guest next weekend," Dima said. "It's rustic, not what she's used to, living in a nice apartment in Milan, near stores for shopping which she loves to do and all of Milan's elegant restaurants."

"Chiara is a bit spoiled, I agree," Valeria said, taking a sip. "But she wants to see us more, not have to take a flight or train trip. We'll be only a couple hours from her."

"We'll see her often, mostly on weekends when she doesn't have a date with a gorgeous Italian man. She's eligible and very attractive.

"Almost as attractive as her mother when I met her in Roma. How many years ago was that?"

She shook her head. "Oh, that was last century, can you believe it?"

"And in this century, we'll be living in Italy again. It's taken us almost three years to find the right place. It is perfect for us, remote, difficult to find, and safe. Our friends in Moscow will never find us."

"Let's not talk about that," Valeria snapped. "Don't spoil our evening."

Dima nodded, gestured to their waiter Silvio, from Parma, watching them from inside. He stepped down onto the outdoor patio, greeted them warmly.

"Buonasera signori, è sempre un piacere rivedervi nel nostro ristorante."

"Buonasera Silvio, è un piacere anche per noi," Valeria said.

"Prego, vi lascio il menu" he said, handing them menus. "Our chef suggests his excellent *pici cacio e pepe* tonight."

"Sì, grazie, prendo il cacio e pepe."

"Molto bene. Per la signora invece?"

She pointed at the menu, "I'll have the veal *scaloppine* and roasted vegetables."

"Very good" said Silvio, "May I ask if you've chosen the wine?"

"I'll go on with the Franciacorta," said Valeria "Maybe you'd like a red?"

"Yes please, I'll pair the *pici* with a Tuscan wine, a bottle of Nobile di Montepulciano will do."

Silvio refilled their glasses, excused himself, heading inside to the kitchen with their order.

Dima sipped his wine, reached for a piece of bread in a basket. "I have to admit, I will miss Bern." Valeria nodded, also took a piece of bread.

"It's a beautiful, historic city with many unique features," Dima said. "the Aare River, all the bridges, gardens and flowers starting to bloom, and the bears in the zoo by the river."

"I won't miss the snow," she corrected. "Switzerland . . . snow, they go together. Almost as much snow as Moscow." She shuddered. "I'm from Calabria, the toe of the Italian boot. We don't see snow unless we go north. I don't like cold weather, I look like a bear when I wear heavy coats, gloves, scarves and boots."

"An Italian bear, I like the image," Dima said, sipping his wine, nibbled on his bread.

"I've had it with snow *caro*, I need sunshine, hot weather, and no freezing rains."

"Snow is in my blood," he smiled. "Even Russians say winters go on too long. Then comes glorious spring. It's like life begins all over — at least until the first snow in October."

She shivered, like she could feel a blast of freezing winter wind from Siberia. "It will be hot where we're going, I can't wait."

"Let's take a last look at the Aare, I'll miss that amazing river," Dima said. They stood, he took her hand and led her to a waist high stone wall looking over the river below. Tall trees lined the river banks, leaves fluttering in a cool wind. Even from that height, they could hear the soothing sound of the Aare rapids flowing over stones, winding around a turn where the river formed a loop around the peninsula of the old city center.

"Beautiful, isn't it?" Dima said, his arm around his wife.

"Yes, but chilly, let's go back to our table, I need my sweater."

When they returned to their table, Silvio came from the kitchen, carrying a tray, setting it on a stand by their table with two platters.

"Ooh, that looks delicious Silvio, thank you," Valeria said.

"The chef knows you're one of our best customers."

"And this is our favorite restaurant in Bern, it's almost like home for me. As you know, I'm from Calabria."

They shared pleasantries with Silvio as he served their dinner, replaced the bread basket with one full of freshly cut bread. When he left, they both started eating, enjoying their food, mellow with the effects of the wine and champagne at home.

"I can't wait to move," Valeria said, slicing into her veal scallopini. After she took her first bite, she sliced the baked potato the size of a tennis ball, and cut small slices of the roasted zucchini, onions, squash, and carrots. They ate in silence for a few moments, then Valeria said, "This such a pleasant way to enjoy our last meal in Berne. But I'm anxious to move into our new home."

Dima rolled his pici pasta, raised it to his mouth. "Yes, so am I. It took us three years to find the right home. It will be quiet in the mountains. No traffic or crowds."

"I can't wait to cook my first meal in my new kitchen —

your choice . . . as long as it's pasta. We have to go shopping for food tomorrow, the refrigerator and cupboards are bare like in a fairy tale."

He smiled, "No worries, darling. We don't have to worry about anything, especially money. We have enough to live for a long time, years and years."

"You need to retire, you've work hard for years. In our new home, you can do what you've always wanted, gardening, planting flowers and vegetables — especially tomatoes and basil — "

"What about garlic?"

"No, we can buy garlic at the market, trust me."

"I'd like to grow fruit trees — lemons, limes, maybe apples and cherries."

"Will there be enough sun?"

"Yes, on the roof after the workmen finish resurfacing and clearing trees so we can get sunlight. Carlo, the gardener in Croce, has seeds for vegetables and small fruit trees. He's bringing fresh soil and compost this week. The security system is installed. I'll turn it on tomorrow when we arrive."

"You've thought of everything dear, remote home, security system. And you'd pass for an Italian, you're fluent with a slight Calabrian accent. And all the weight you've lost, almost 30 pounds. Your beard makes you look like a scholar. You wear only Italian clothes — suits, shoes, and that funny beret, even though Italian men don't wear berets."

At the end of the evening, their bottles of wine empty, as well as two glasses of grappa. Not a crumb of tiramisu left on either plate.

After paying with a credit card, Dima left two 100 Euro bills in an envelope on the table for Silvio, who caught their eye as they walked toward the door. Valeria and Dima waved, Silvio bowed. They said parting words, hugged, and said good bye.

Silvio's last words were, "*Buon viaggio.*"

"I'm going to miss Silvio," Valeria said as Dima opened the door for her, a gush of chilly April evening breeze ruffling her hair. "Thanks for leaving a generous tip."

Dima tugged his coat collar close to his neck, shivering in the chilly night air. "He's a gentleman, I'll miss him too."

They walked down the tile steps to the stone driveway, Dima's arm around her shoulder, she grabbing his hand. She said, "I wonder what Silvio will think when we don't show up next Sunday? Pity we couldn't tell him."

"No one has a hint that we're leaving, except the supervisor at our apartment. I left a forwarding address in Moscow, nothing about where we were really going."

"But Silvio, what about him?"

"I took care of that. In the note with the tip, I told him we'd be away for a few weeks so he won't think we're going to another restaurant."

"That's nice, thank you. I'll miss him, he was always nice to us."

They reached Kornhausestrasse arm in arm, the wind rustling the pine trees along the street. They followed streetlights to their apartment, reminiscing about their good times in Bern, almost four years. But that was over now.

When they reached their apartment, Dima opened the gate by pressing the code to open it.

"Last night in our apartment," Dima said. "I'm a bit nostalgic."

"Me too, I guess," she said, her voice trailing off as they pushed the door into the apartment building. "Tomorrow we sleep in Italia. I'm so happy."

www.ingramcontent.com/pod-product-compliance
Lightning Source LLC
Chambersburg PA
CBHW061100100726
47911CB00012B/315